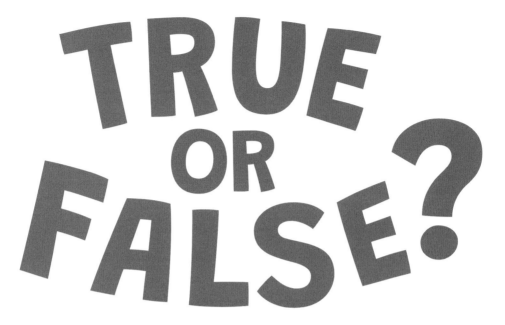

TRUE OR FALSE?

The Science of Perception, Misinformation, and Disinformation

Jacqueline B. Toner, PhD

MAGINATION PRESS • WASHINGTON, DC

AMERICAN PSYCHOLOGICAL ASSOCIATION

DEDICATION

This book was written with my darlings in
mind. For Henry, Julian, Lilly, and Margo—JT

Magination Press is a registered trademark of the American Psychological Association. Order
books at maginationpress.org or call 1-800-374-2721.

Book design by Collaborate Agency, Ltd.
Printed by Sonic Media Solutions, Inc., Medford, NY

Library of Congress Cataloging-in-Publication Data
Names: Toner, Jacqueline B., author.
Title: True or false? : the science of perception, misinformation, and disinformation / by
Jacqueline B. Toner.
Description: [Washington, D.C.]: Magination Press, [2024] | Includes bibliographical references
and index. | Summary: "The psychology of processes which contribute to the development and
persistence of false perceptions and beliefs and the difficulty of correcting them"—Provided
by publisher.
Identifiers: LCCN 2023027967 (print) | LCCN 2023027968 (ebook) | ISBN 9781433840487
(hardcover) | ISBN 9781433840494 (ebook)
Subjects: LCSH: Information behavior—Psychological aspects—Juvenile literature. |
Information literacy—Psychological aspects—Juvenile literature. | Errors—Psychological
aspects—Juvenile literature. | Truthfulness and falsehood—Psychological aspects—Juvenile
literature.
Classification: LCC BF444 .T66 2024 (print) | LCC BF444 (ebook) | DDC 153—dc23/eng/20231107
| LC record available at https://lccn.loc.gov/2023027967 | LC ebook record available at https://
lccn.loc.gov/2023027968

Manufactured in the United States

10 9 8 7 6 5 4 3 2 1

TABLE OF CONTENTS

A Note for the Adults in Your Life

The importance of fostering critical thinking is often emphasized when speaking of the educational needs of children in middle and high school. Definitions of critical thinking vary but most focus on a number of different cognitive skills, including the ability to analyze information and think rationally about it. Whatever the definition, the goal is to help students develop a questioning approach to information so that they can arrive at an unbiased judgement about its accuracy.

Not an easy task! I have shared some of what psychologists have learned about how we are fooled into believing things that simply aren't true. Our own cognitive processes, attention, and emotions sometimes interfere with perception and clear thinking. Prior knowledge can distort our understanding of new information. And then, there is the problem of misinformation and disinformation.

How do we protect kids (and ourselves) from making poor judgements about what is accurate and what is not? As is discussed towards the end of the book, research has shown that the most effective protection against disinformation is "prebunking," a warning that false information is coming, who is presenting it, and why.

Of course, we can't anticipate all the false messages our children (or we) will encounter, and prebunking is not always an option. I think of this book as what I will call "procedural prebunking," or presenting facts (as well as they are currently understood) about the ways in which we humans come to misunderstand things. My hope is that by drawing back the curtain and shedding light on the process of misunderstanding, kids can become more effective critical thinkers.

Good luck!
Jacqueline B. Toner, PhD

When the World Was Flat

Quiz Time!

Have a look at the following statements. Which do you think are true and which are false?

- Tomatoes are poisonous.
- People only use ten percent of their brains.
- A ten-year-old Twinkie is still fresh enough to eat.
- Cold weather means that global warming is fake.
- Reading in the dark ruins your eyes.
- Bulls get angry when they see red.
- Bats are blind.
- Dogs sweat with their tongues.
- Swimming after eating causes cramps.
- Lightning never strikes the same place twice.
- Earth is flat.

Turns out they are all false. If you believed some of them, that's okay. You are not alone! Lots of people are fooled when wrong information is passed from person to person. Sometimes that wrong information fools a lot of people, even most people, for a long time. Even years and years!

You may have heard that, until Columbus set out on his exploration, people believed the Earth was flat. Not so much. The ancient Greek philosopher, Aristotle, not only believed Earth was a sphere, but shared his evidence more than 2,000 years ago! While some people may have continued to think the Earth was flat, most educated people did not. Christopher Columbus certainly knew the planet was round before he set out on his explorations. Yet, for generations, children have been led to believe (by adults who believe it) that people during Columbus's time were sure he would sail off the edge of the flat Earth.

That's not the only thing people believe because "everyone knows it's true." At one time or another you've probably been told by an adult to put on a coat so you won't catch a cold. But cold weather doesn't cause colds, viruses do. Although people tend to get more colds during winter, it has nothing to do with the weather. It happens because, when it is cold, people spend more time inside close to other people (and their germs).

Both misunderstandings (as well as many more) have been shared, believed, and passed on by lots of people. How does such a thing happen? As you'll learn more about later, hearing the same (wrong) idea over and over can make it seem true. It can also make it seem that everyone believes it.

In the pages of this book, you will read about how false beliefs come about and why they tend to stick. You will also discover how misunderstanding, and misuse of scientific findings can lead people to the wrong conclusions and cause lots of problems. Once you know all this, you will be less likely to be fooled by things you hear, read, and see that aren't true. Dig in and learn how to separate fact from fake!

Imperfect Minds: The Science of Perception and Misunderstanding

You are an amazing thinker. Our world is filled with sights, sounds, and other sensations, but you can focus on what matters most. You recognize patterns and relationships quickly and easily. You make comparisons to things you already know, often without even realizing it. You simplify new information and tie it to older stuff you already know, which helps you remember it and recall it later.

But this efficiency comes with some built-in glitches. Our quick and automatic thinking can put us at risk of making errors. Those mistakes can even fool us into believing things that aren't true.

In Part One, we will explore what psychologists have uncovered about our thinking strategies. We'll look at how those skills can lead to distorted beliefs. Learning what we, as humans, tend to overlook or cast aside can help us make fewer mistakes about what we really "know."

CHAPTER 1

Can You Believe It?

Your science teacher just gave you an assignment to find out how the brain understands what a person sees and hears. You head to the library and search for information in the biology and psychology sections. After browsing through books for an hour, a friend walks in and says, "What is the color of the book second from the right on the top shelf of the room you just left?"

You give them a weird look, then shrug. "It's red," they say. And you believe them, but you wonder. You certainly saw that book, so why don't you know the answer?

There is a lot going on in this situation, so let's start from the beginning, with your senses.

When someone says something that doesn't match your experience, you might protest, "But I saw it with my own eyes!" It makes sense to think you can believe things you've personally seen or heard. But what you experienced isn't the whole story. The information that comes through your senses is just the first step. Next, your brain has to interpret that information. That's called perception. It happens super quickly and most of the time your brain does a pretty good job. But sometimes, its fast speed and built-in shortcuts can cause errors. In fact, human brains can be a little glitchy, as you'll read about in this chapter. Seriously, your brain isn't a computer. It can make processing errors! Let's take a closer look, starting with your **senses**.

Senses/Sensory organs: our five senses are sight, hearing, touch, taste, and smell. Information is collected through sensory organs (eyes, ears, skin and pressure sensors, taste buds, and nose) and sent to the brain for interpretation.

Slam! I **hear** the oven door close. I **see** something brown. It **feels** warm. It **smells** yummy. It **tastes** sweet. It's a brownie!

See It, Hear It, Feel It, Know It?

We all know our senses never lie, right? Well, sort of. While our senses don't lie, our brain can misinterpret what we see, hear, or feel, and fill in gaps to get to something more familiar, safe, or comfortable.

Look at this drawing. Is it a circle? Most people would say it is. But look again. A circle is a continuous curved line, but this drawing shows three curved lines that aren't connected to each other.

Although we talk about "seeing" with our eyes, the process is more complicated. Eyes are **sensory organs**. Like all sensory organs, they take in information from the environment, then send signals to your brain. Next, your brain has to make sense of what you experienced.

Pay Attention!

Maybe you've had a teacher or a parent remind you to

pay Attention!

Of course, when that happens the person asking you to pay attention wants you to pay attention to something specific, like a classmate during their book report or your dad explaining board game rules during family game night.

But it's impossible to pay attention to everything around you all the time. You pay close attention to some things and ignore others. You need to be able to ignore some things or you would be overwhelmed—your brain can't possibility record everything it sees! You might be surprised by what your brain "sees" and doesn't see.

CHECK OUT THE RESEARCH

In a very famous experiment, Daniel Simons and Christopher Chabris showed just how extreme errors can be when we aren't paying 100% attention. They asked students to watch a video of people passing a basketball and to count the number of passes between people wearing white shirts. Only half of the people watching the video noticed when a person in a gorilla suit walked through the group, beating their chest. Dr. Simon and Dr. Chabris labeled this phenomenon **inattentional blindness or selective attention**. Search online for "Gorillas in Our Midst," to see the actual video used in the experiment. Hard to believe, but it is true!

Try This

Don't turn the page. Remember the drawing of the library in the beginning of this chapter? How many kids were there? Were they sitting at a table or on the floor? Did the librarian have her hair in a ponytail? What animal was on the front of one kid's t-shirt? Was there a blue book on the second shelf?

If you are unsure of any of these details, it isn't because your eyes failed to see them. It's because they didn't seem important, so you didn't pay attention to them.

Inattentional blindness: the failure to see something that is clearly visible because attention is focused on another activity or object.

What Did You See?

Some scientists estimate that 90% of the information we see never gets to our brains. We focus on the big things, the general impressions, the stuff that seems important, and miss most of the details. That means sometimes your brain has to guess and fill in gaps about what you saw, based on other kinds of information. That other information might include your past experiences or your understanding of how things work. So, when you see something new, your brain interprets what you saw and mixes it all together with what you already knew to form a **perception**. A perception is your understanding or way of thinking about something you experienced.

One set of shortcuts your brain uses to form perceptions is based on what it knows about shapes. Scientists refer to these as Gestalt principles. You've already seen an example of how your brain connected a set of curved, but unattached, lines to form a circle. That's a **Gestalt principle** called the **closure principle**.

Perception: the recognition and interpretation of sensory information.

Gestalt principles: laws that describe how humans recognize patterns, simplify images, and group information to aid in perception of objects. Like the **closure principle** that says we fill in a set of curved, but unattached, lines to form a circle.

DID YOU KNOW?

The word "Gestalt" means "shape" in German.
Another Gestalt principle called the **law of continuity** states that we tend to see broken lines as unbroken. So, you probably see this picture as two crossing lines and not a bunch of dots.

You might know that pictures on a computer screen are made of pixels, small dots or squares that form an image. Our brains combine these small bits into a single picture, an example of Gestalt principles in action!

All this filling-in and neatening of perceptions usually works well. But sometimes your brain's shortcuts can lead to errors. This is called **misperception**—a mistaken or untrue impression about something. Misperceptions are very common and can cause problems. They might lead you to jump to conclusions, develop misunderstandings, or even have false memories!

Misperception: a mistaken or untrue impression about something.

Try This

Look at the clouds in the sky. What do you see? Our brains look for shapes that are familiar. If we sense something that appears to be like a recognizable object but is missing parts, our brains fill in the pieces. If things seem similar or are close together, we put them in the same group. Our brains prefer things tidy and simple! This cleaning up of messy, incoming information happens quickly and automatically, without our awareness. And it all comes together into something that makes sense to your brain. That's a perception!

DID YOU KNOW?

How your body feels can influence perceptions in weird and interesting ways. For example, if you are carrying a heavy backpack, the hill in front of you will seem steeper.

Want to make that climb easier? Imagine your BFF. Turns out that just thinking about a good friend can make a hill seem less steep!

Jumping to Conclusions

The Tasmanian tiger was a dog-like marsupial that once lived in Australia. As far as anyone knows, the last Tasmanian tiger died in 1936. But recently, someone "saw" one. This is a picture of the last one thought to be alive.

Now, imagine you've been searching for this creature in the wild when you come upon a partially hidden animal that looks like this.

See the animal partly hidden behind leaves? Its fur color, ear shape, and long snout look like what you would see on a Tasmanian tiger, right? The photographer actually believed they had discovered an animal thought to be extinct for over 80 years! Had this creature been avoiding humans all these years? Or was someone's brain playing tricks on them? Can you imagine how a person who has looked at many pictures of a Tasmanian tiger, and who believes they may still exist in the wild, might fill in the missing parts of this view and interpret this as a Tasmanian tiger?

Actually, the second animal is a Tasmanian pandemelon, an Australian marsupial that looks more like a kangaroo or wallaby (animals that are very much NOT extinct) than a Tasmanian tiger.

Our brains were not meant to function in towns, cities, or even modern country places. You know, the settings in which we now live. We have brains that developed in an environment filled with threats of predators, the need for instant awareness of danger, and the ability to make fast decisions to ensure survival. Relying on quick reactions of fear and instantaneous decisions kept our ancestors alive on the savannas of the past.

Unfortunately, those same instantaneous, sometimes emotion-driven choices don't always work as well in our current living situations. While we may be tempted to rely on those ancient impulses, it can make us vulnerable to false conclusions and beliefs. Often, we need to put aside our first impressions and think twice (or even three times) to make the best decisions. It can help to be aware of the types of errors we, as humans, tend to make as we reconsider our initial understanding. It is more time consuming and effortful, but it may save us from drawing faulty conclusions and believing things that aren't true.

Filling in Gaps Is Useful

Why would human brains make these kinds of mistakes? Well, although filling in gaps can sometimes lead to errors, at other times it's very helpful. This kind of educated guessing applies to what we hear as well as what we see. When we listen to someone talk, there's often lots of background noise and interruptions making it difficult to hear what is said. You might miss a word or part of a word here or there (and not just when a parent is telling you to do your chores!). By filling in those blanks, you can understand what the person is saying.

In the early days of texting, people were limited in the number of characters (letters, numbers, and symbols) they could include in a message. So people created shortcuts by taking out letters from words, like NVM, UR, RLY, and ABT, or shortening phrases to the first letter in each word, like SMH, LOL, BRB, and TTYL. People naturally fill in gaps in words and still understand what someone is trying to say. You probably have little difficulty understanding this message, despite the missing letters.

Tht wsn't hrd! LOL

CHECK OUT THE RESEARCH

Makio Kashino had people listen to recordings of words with some sounds missing. He also had them try to understand recordings with background noise that hid parts of a word. Their brains were still able to understand what they heard! Clever human brains can fill in missing parts of speech based on what they expect to be there. Amazing, huh?

Try This

Write a short message but leave out all the vowels. Hand it to a parent, friend, or other "research subject." Are they able to read it?

It Ought To Be There, So It Was!

You already know that your brain fills in gaps in what you see and hear. But what about memory? Do we remember stuff we expected would be there even if it isn't? It turns out we do! Once again, those human brains are a bit glitchy!

CHECK OUT THE RESEARCH

Psychologists William Brewer and James Treyens had people wait briefly in an office. After they left the room, the people were asked to remember everything they had seen there. Almost everyone said they'd seen things that would commonly be in an office: a desk, chairs, etc. About a third of them also said they saw books. But there were no books! The research participants had filled in gaps in their memory with what they expected would be in an office.

Think back to how we started this chapter. Let's think more closely about your friend, the library, and that red book. While you were in the library your eyes probably passed over every single book as you were searching for the books you actually wanted. So why couldn't you answer your friend's question about the color of the book on the top shelf in the room you'd just left? In fact, your eyes see many details all around you which your brain chooses to ignore. (By the way, did you notice the kid with the gorilla shirt—hahaha?) In fact, if you paid attention to what color each book in a library was it would be very distracting, and no work would get done. Your brain was just being efficient!

A Little Help From Your Friends (and Strangers)

What's the big deal? It's not like you need to know all the colors of all the books in the library! When your friend suggests the book is red, you agree. Easy. After you realize you missed something, you may rely on later clues to figure out what you missed. Sometimes, even if you did see something, learning what someone else thinks can change what you think you saw. Sometimes those clues come from other people, even if what they say is incorrect. For example, learning that your friend saw mostly blue books in the library can change what you think you saw, even if you saw only red books in the library! And, what other people say may or may not be correct!

What difference does all this make? Imagine that somebody broke into a car. If more than one person is at the scene of the crime, they may talk about it as they wait for the police to arrive. If later they are called as eyewitnesses, they may agree about what happened, even if they didn't have the same point of view or notice the same details as they witnessed the break-in. This can be a problem because juries tend to think people who were at the scene of a crime are believable. Eyewitnesses have a powerful influence on whether someone is convicted of a crime and sent to prison, or found innocent and set free.

People assume memory is a perfect recording of what happened. But people miss details all the time! In fact, scientists have shown that eyewitness testimony isn't very reliable after all. In recent years, DNA evidence has been used to demonstrate that some people who have been found guilty were actually innocent. In some cases, it was because eyewitnesses did not actually see what they thought they had seen.

And it's not only witnesses to crimes that have faulty memories. Research suggests that having your memory change because of what someone else says they saw happens to us all!

CHECK OUT THE RESEARCH

To better understand how other people's comments can change a person's memory, a team of researchers led by Maryanne Garry had pairs of participants watch a video together. Everyone watched the same video, but one person in each pair wore special glasses that changed what was visible to them.

In the video a workman went through an empty house and took some things. The people with the glasses saw eight details that their partners didn't (because of those special glasses). Later, the pairs took a memory test together. If some of those eight details were talked about, the people who couldn't see those eight details (again, because of the glasses) said they had. So, just hearing that someone saw something can change your memory of what you saw! How weird is that!

Try This

Consider how a witness's memory of seeing someone flee a crime scene might change if they see a report about the event on internet or social media or read about it in a newspaper? What if they learned the person being charged with the crime had been convicted of similar crimes in the past and had just been released from jail? Now consider how their memory might be different if the report said the individual ran a very successful business in the neighborhood, had never been in any trouble, and was organizing local kids to pick up trash in a park. Can you see why judges ask potential jurors if they have been following media reports of the crime in question?

Human brains are great at processing a lot of information to make quick decisions. This can be a plus, but it can also lead to problems and fool us into believing we have had experiences when we haven't. Or we might jump to conclusions that are just plain wrong. Or misinterpret what's right in front of us. Keep a look out for ways in which your own perception gets things wrong sometimes. It may save you from believing things that aren't true.

Now You Know

- Perception is your brain's interpretation of information gathered from your senses (sight, sound, smell, taste, and touch).

- Your brain reviews your past experiences and understanding of how the world works, along with clues from immediate surroundings and other people, to interpret information from your senses.

- Because the brain is so efficient and makes these interpretations very fast, you might end up with a misperception (false belief or misunderstanding).

CHAPTER 2

Who Is Believable?

Your friend tells you that walking backwards can improve your soccer game. Sounds strange but possible, so you decide to check it out. You do an online search and find an article from a doctor who says walking backwards improves balance. You also find a statement by an actor who is into backward walking and says it helped her do some of her own stunts in a recent action film.

   With all these sources and "proof," are you convinced?

Who Do We Trust?

When it comes to backward walking, the **sources** you found explaining what a great exercise it is might convince you to try it. When we hear new information, we consider how people we trust think about it. If you're like most people, you probably trust someone who is a friend, a classmate, or someone in your family.

But other people can also have a strong influence on what you believe. It probably won't surprise you to learn that when people don't know anything about a subject, they tend to be convinced by those who have special knowledge about it. In other words, they turn to an expert. Not only are expert opinions valued, but listeners' brains respond differently to expert opinions than to those from nonexperts.

> **Source:** where something comes from. This can include a person, news article, book, or video that provides information.

CHECK OUT THE RESEARCH

Dar Meshi and research colleagues used **functional magnetic resonance imaging (fMRI)** to record what was happening in people's brains after they listened to expert advice about a decision. They compared that brain activity to what happened when people listened to nonexperts.

While listening to the expert, certain parts of the brain became more active. And get this, the parts that got fired up were areas that also become active when we look forward to getting rewards. In this case, the "reward" was getting good information. The experiment found that people were more likely to listen to what those experts had to say.

> **Functional magnetic resonance imagery (fMRI):** brain imagery that uses magnetic technology to map brain activity.

Your brain is very complex! It is responsible for everything you do—running, singing, jumping, dreaming, thinking, reading this book—everything. It is also very organized with different areas designed to control certain things.
Here's what's inside:

Frontal lobe:
This part helps you make decisions, remember things, talk, and keeps you motivated to do stuff.

Parietal lobe:
This part processes all the sensations you feel.

Occipital lobe:
This part is important for vision and processing visual images.

This portion of the brain gets all fired up by expert advice.

Temporal lobe:
This part is crucial for hearing, processing sounds, learning, and memory.

Brain stem:
This area serves as an important relay location between your brain and the rest of your body. It regulates many functions needed for life, like breathing and heart rate, and helps coordinate movement like walking or playing video games!

Cerebellum:
This part controls our body position, balance, and coordination.

It makes sense to listen to someone who has special knowledge about something. But it isn't just experts who are more easily believed. Celebrities can have an even bigger influence on beliefs than experts. This is true even when the topic is something they know little about. A study by Steven Arnocky and others found people were more convinced that evolution was true when they heard about it from a movie star than from a scientist!

Some actors and athletes have stated they believe the Earth is flat. Earth science experts have responded that not only would that make it hard to explain gravity but direct observations from space have revealed the Earth as a sphere.

You might be thinking:

Wait! What?

Advertisers understand the power of famous folks. That's why film stars, music idols, and athletes are used to convince us to buy all kinds of stuff. If an expert says they think walking backwards helps with athletic performance, research suggests you'll take that information seriously. Learning that a celebrity you admire practices backward walking might just make you a true believer!

The Problem With Testimonials

A close friend tells you they don't believe living off junk food is bad for you. After all, they never touch a vegetable or fruit and the only meat they eat is a daily hot dog. They point out they are perfectly healthy. They didn't even get the cold that was going around last week! Would you join them in feasting only on potato chips and soda?

Hopefully you've heard about healthy food choices from other people you trust, and won't just go along with your friend. Sometimes **testimonials** can lead you to make poor choices. While testimonials can come from people you know, they sometimes come from celebrities or other famous people. But a testimonial is just the person's report about their own experience. They may have no information about how something affected others. They are assuming that if it's true for them, it's true for everyone. Be careful! It might not be. Based just on one person's experience, there's no way to know. Taking one example as proof for everyone, everywhere, all the time is called **generalization** and can lead to false beliefs.

> **Testimonial:** a person's report about the value or usefulness of something.

> **Generalization:** a conclusion that something is true in most cases. It's not wise to make generalizations based on evidence from one or a few specific cases.

Generalizations	
Everyone	assumption that if it's true for one, it's true for all situations
Everywhere	assumption that if it happened in one situation, in one place, it's true in all situations
All the Time	assumption that if it happened once, it will always happen

Think about the junk food example. What might your friend be overlooking? Consider the three types of generalizations you have learned:

1. Other people. Might someone else have a different experience?
2. Other factors. Is diet the only influence on health?
3. Time frame. Is this week the only week to decide how healthy they are?

For another example about how generalizations work, we often rely on friends' advice when choosing "the best" movies, clubs to join, things to buy, and even teachers, even though our friends' experiences are limited. While they may like certain books or music, they've only read or listened to a small amount of what's actually out there. They have hit it off with their guitar teacher, but that teacher's style may not fit with what you need. Have you ever followed a friend's recommendation but found you didn't like something as much as they thought you would?

Facts or Opinion?

When you hear information it's important to know whether it's an **opinion** or **fact**. Facts can come from different kinds of sources, but what they have in common is information that is **evidence-based**. That means there is data to support it. That data may come from a scientific study, or it may come from an investigation by a journalist, a historian, or other expert. Opinions are simply a person's thoughts about something. Facts are based on evidence and always supported by data.

Opinion: a thought or judgement that isn't based on evidence.

Fact: a conclusion based on evidence.

Evidence-based: conclusions based on systematic methods of data collection. Often, this is through a collection of scientific studies.

DID YOU KNOW?

A fact is...

- something that can be tested or proven
- based on research or careful observation
- true in most cases
- supported by evidence

An opinion is...

- someone's thoughts or judgement which can't be proven or disproven
- based on personal experience or view
- true in one case, but maybe not others
- supported by argument

People who use evidence to back up what they say are more **reliable** sources. Researchers follow guidelines to check the accuracy of the data they collect. Investigative reporters seek more than one source of evidence and check and recheck what they learn. Historians look at many kinds of records to gather data about events of the past.

Reliable: a person or information that is trustworthy.

Experts Have Limits

Even someone who is an expert isn't an expert on everything. Before deciding to believe an expert, ask yourself if their area of special knowledge relates to the subject they are speaking about. For instance, a doctor has a lot of medical knowledge, but they may not be the best person to give advice on playing better basketball. On the other hand, you wouldn't ask your basketball coach whether the pain in your stomach means you need to have your appendix removed, right? While those examples are pretty obvious, you'll soon learn how easily people are fooled by others who know a lot about one thing, but not the thing they're talking about!

Try This

A basketball coach is an expert on basketball techniques, a doctor on aches and pains, a historian on facts of the past. What source would you turn to if you:

- needed help with a broken water pipe
- needed help with math homework
- were trying to learn to cook
- wanted to know about whether something was against the law
- wanted to find out facts about Mars
- wanted to know what the weather would be like tomorrow
- wanted to know how to fix your computer
- wanted to learn facts about giraffes

Where Did I Hear That?

Just as we can't pay attention to everything around us, we can't remember everything we experience. We forget things we're not reminded of over time, things we didn't think were important to remember, and lots more. In fact, humans forget a lot! Have you ever repeated a story but forgot who told it to you? That happens to everyone. When we forget where information came from, we may also forget who the source was. When we forget the source, we may think it was someone more reliable than is true.

Did I learn that elephants can swim on a nature show, or did I see it on a cartoon?

If you forget where you heard something, you might make a guess about the source and if it's trustworthy information. Research shows we can even be fooled into thinking the source was us! "No way!" you say? Read on!

CHECK OUT THE RESEARCH

Could you be fooled into thinking you'd had an adventure when you hadn't? A study by psychologist Kimberly Wade and others found that changing digital images could change people's memories of their own experiences.

Adult research participants were shown pictures of themselves as kids, in a hot air balloon. But the pictures weren't real. They had never taken that ride. The researchers had digitally added the participants to childhood pictures, replacing pictures of strangers enjoying a ride in a hot air balloon. Later, the people were asked about past experiences. Half of the people shared "memories" of the hot air balloon ride they had never taken!

Real World Impact

During the COVID-19 pandemic, people had a hard time knowing who to believe and what information to trust. This confusion was made worse by seemingly conflicting information from scientists and doctors in the early days of the crisis. Messages changed as scientists began to learn more about the disease and how best to control its spread.

Some people understood this was just how science works: early research may indicate one thing, but further studies result in different conclusions. But other people started to wonder if the experts weren't so expert after all.

Some people became more willing to believe false information from those who seemed more confident than scientists. Since people were very worried, they talked to friends and family about the virus a lot. This meant false information was spread quickly.

The confusion about who to believe led to many people ignoring what experts said about avoiding crowds and wearing masks. As a result, more people became ill and even died than would have if everyone had listened to this advice early in the pandemic.

You've read about how getting information from conflicting sources interfered with developing needed solutions for a serious problem. But restricting sources of information can also stop new ideas from being shared. That's why the founders of our country supported free speech, so people would be able to hear ideas from lots of places.

What might happen if an authoritarian head of state or the leader of a cult (people who tightly control what others hear) blocked sources that provide information critical of the "facts" they wanted people to believe?

When trying to decide whether something is true, consider the source. Is the message coming from a source you trust? Is information based on fact or opinion? Does the source have evidence to support the ideas they are presenting?

Now You Know

- Although experts are often seen as trusted sources of information, messages from celebrities are also easily trusted.

- Testimonials are a less reliable source of information than conclusions based on scientific evidence.

- A single person's experience may or may not reflect what is true for other people at different times or in different circumstances.

- Humans are prone to forgetting where information came from and whether or not it was reliable.

CHAPTER 3

Does It Make a Good Story?

About 60 years ago, a California newspaper reported that construction workers found giant footprints while building a road. The footprints looked like human footprints but were much larger than even the biggest person would make. The newspaper imagined the footprints had come from a giant creature they named "Bigfoot."

Even before these footprints were reported, Native Americans had passed down stories or **myths** about "Sasquatches," giant human-like creatures who roamed the Pacific Northwest.

Myth: an idea, often in the form of a story, that is widely believed but untrue. Myths are sometimes repeated through generations.

Since then, people from every state except Hawaii have reported Bigfoot sightings or signs of the creature. In 1967 two men claimed they had film of a large, hairy-looking giant walking on two legs. It turned out their film was a fake. In 1970 a Bigfoot hunter claimed he had samples of the creature's hair and skin, which he sent to the FBI for testing. The FBI said the samples probably came from a deer.

Although it is almost impossible to prove something doesn't exist, it seems unlikely an animal as large as Bigfoot could hide for half a century. Especially when people were hunting for it. Even though the evidence doesn't support it, there are still people who believe in the myth of Bigfoot.

DID YOU KNOW?

Bigfoot isn't the only myth about an enormous but hard to spot creature. For many years people have searched for the Loch Ness Monster. Some even thought it might be a leftover dinosaur. So far, evidence for its existence has been unconvincing, but the myth lives on.

Sometimes myths are based on a bit of fact that has changed or been elaborated. Take the case of the unicorn. A recent fossil discovery showed that an extinct one-horned animal, which looked a bit like a rhinoceros, lived during prehistoric human times. It didn't look like the unicorns we see today, covered with rainbows and sparkles, but could a one-horned creature like this have inspired stories that were passed down thousands of years?

EXPLORE FURTHER

You can see just how fake the film footage of Bigfoot looks by searching, "Bigfoot, 1967" online. Would you have been fooled by this?

Why Is It So Tempting To Believe Myths?

We are more likely to believe something if it's in the form of an entertaining story. Let's face it, Bigfoot, the Loch Ness monster, and unicorns are fun! Simple stories with unexpected bits are easier for people to remember and accept than long, complicated ones. What could be more fun to hear about than the story of a giant, hairy creature hidden away for years? You probably wouldn't forget it. In fact, you'd probably share it with your friends!

Of course, the more a story is simplified, the more details are left out and the further it strays from the truth. To make a story flow smoothly, details that don't fit are left out. And interesting tidbits that aren't true may be added to make things more engaging.

We know from scientific research that when information is passed from person to person, it changes. And those changes aren't random. Messages change in ways that grab the listener's attention and are easy to remember. Thomas Gilovich refers to this as **sharpening** (focusing on the main parts of the story) and **leveling** (cutting out details that seem less important). He discovered that sharpening and leveling make stories not only easier to remember, but also more extreme.

Sharpening: the process of focusing on the most interesting parts of a story and leaving out details.

Leveling: the process of simplifying details of a story to make it easier to remember.

Thomas Gilovich researched how **secondhand information** leads to simpler but more extreme messages. He used pairs of friends in his study. One person knew a third person that their partner had only heard about.

The researcher asked both to describe the third person. The partner who had only heard about the third person gave more exaggerated descriptions.

Secondhand information: information that is learned from someone else.

They Saw It Themselves!

All information is not treated equally by human brains. The kind of information, and the way it's presented, can change whether we accept it or not.

We sometimes hear things from other people as an **anecdote**, a report of their own experience. Anecdotes are often told as a story about something that happened to a person. To "help" the listener, the person telling the anecdote focuses on unusual aspects of the story to make it more interesting.

Anecdote: a person's report about one experience.

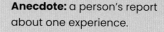

They emphasize parts to make a point, focus on dramatic details, or make it seem as if they were more involved than they really were. All of this makes the story more interesting, but less true!

All of these changes are common. They don't happen because the person is trying to fool their listener; they just want to tell a good story. But these changes in focus change meaning and can lead to the listener believing things that aren't completely true.

Try This

Families pass down stories that are repeated year after year. They may be shared when relatives gather at holidays or family events. Think about your family stories. Do any of them seem exaggerated? Are there details that don't seem possible? Do the stories show a family member's personality in a way that seems more extreme than the way you see them? Does it appear the story is a way of making a person seem good (or bad, or silly, or smart, or brave, or clever, or lucky)?

When Grandpa was fishing in Alaska last summer, he caught enough salmon for 20 people, every single day!

When you hear someone talk about an experience, you probably believe them. After all, they're talking about something that happened to them. Surely, they know what happened! It can be especially easy to accept someone's story if it's exciting. But all self-reported stories include the speaker's own misperceptions and distortions. Although they may be doing their best to tell the truth, their story contains errors. Errors they may not be aware of. You can guess they probably missed important details or didn't see them as important. They may have made assumptions about why things happened and added details which fit those ideas. When we hear first-person accounts, it's easy to forget this is only one person's experience. But if it makes a good story, it's easy to believe.

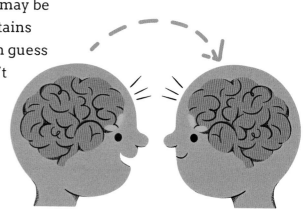

Speaker   **Listener**

CHECK OUT THE RESEARCH

Neuropsychologist Uri Hasson and colleagues studied how storytellers and their listeners' brains become "aligned." They had people watch an episode of a TV show. Those participants then told other people what happened in the show. Brain scans showed the listener's brain waves looked similar to the speaker's when they'd watched the show.

When you hear about someone else's experience your brain reacts as if you were with them when it happened.

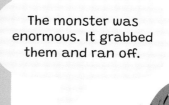

The monster was enormous. It grabbed them and ran off.

Believing Is Easier Than Not Believing

Okay, back to these kind of efficient (and sometimes lazy) human brains of ours! One reason we sometimes believe things that aren't true is that it's just plain easier. When we hear something, we assume it's true. In fact, to make sense of it we need to accept it and roll it around in our brains a bit. Once we believe it, it takes extra work to decide it's not true. So, it's easier to believe the first thing you hear and ignore anything that challenges it later. When it comes to figuring out what is true or not, humans are built to take the easy road, and rethinking something we've decided is correct requires extra work!

I'm sure it's true. Don't bother me!

Glarks have brown fur is false.

Glarks have brown fur is....true

CHECK OUT THE RESEARCH

Daniel Gilbert and his research team had research participants read about an imaginary creature called a glark and remember all they could about this furry animal. Before being tested on these glark facts, people read questions in advance to make sure they understood what would be asked. Unbeknown to the participant, true and false statements about glarks were included in the test. This part of the experiment was designed to have participants see and understand the false information.

The result? When tested about their knowledge of glarks, just reading and thinking about false statements made it more likely people thought they were true.

It seems simply understanding something makes it stick in our minds. This can confuse us into thinking we've made a decision based on facts.

I've Heard That Before

Why do you see and hear the same advertisements over and over? Shouldn't just one ad be enough to convince you to buy (or watch or eat) something if it's a good something? Well, people pushing those somethings know a bit about psychological research. It turns out that hearing something again and again can be enough to fool us into believing it. That includes believing that the something being advertised is the best kind of something there is!

Think about it. If you have a cold, chances are you'll want some Kleenex. But stop for a second! "Kleenex" isn't an object. It's the name of one brand of facial tissues. Through many years of hearing the brand connected to the object, "Kleenex" has come to mean the thing itself. And if someone asked you to choose, you'd probably say Kleenex makes the best tissue. Maybe, but it's just as likely that Kleenex is simply the most familiar. Kleenex is an example of very successful branding. Of course, promoting brands is what advertising is all about.

Cloudy soft

Kleenex

Search your brain (and house). What things can you identify that are called by their brand name? You could start with these:

☐ plastic cushioning wrap that has air pockets

☐ plastic shoes

☐ small sticks with a bit of a cotton ball at each end

☐ permanent markers

☐ a plastic disc used to play catch

☐ a plastic circle a person can spin around their hips (well...some can!)

☐ bits of paper that temporarily stick to other paper

☐ small bandages that can be stuck over cuts

☐ plastic food containers

☐ vehicles that smooth the ice at an icerink

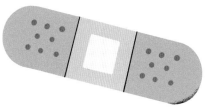

(Answers are at the end of the chapter!)

Our (sometimes overly) efficient brains accept that if something sounds like something we've heard before, it's probably true. Familiarity can make us skip the hard work of critical thinking. This happens even if we have no evidence. This is called **familiarity bias** and means we may believe something just because we recognize it from before.

Familiarity bias: when we accept familiar ideas without careful thought about their accuracy.

Advertisers know how comfortable we all can get when something is familiar to us. They sometimes pay to have their products show up in movies or other entertainment. The "product placement" of a drink, snack food, or clothing brand makes it more familiar to viewers. Even when nothing is said about it, people may buy that product simply because they've seen it before. So next time you grab a new type of soda, you might be doing so because of familiarity bias!

Information that's repeated is even more likely to be believed if it's presented quickly. Rapid presentation makes it harder to think things through critically. This happens a lot online. Since information presented in internet sidebars and ads is often quick and repeated over and over, it can be very effective at making ideas seem familiar, and of convincing us of false information.

Real World Impact

Although journalists strive to report facts truthfully, they also need to tell a good story. To do so, they focus on exciting details and sometimes skip over those less likely to grab the audience's attention. News outlets are often criticized for not sharing enough "good news." But good news can be boring. People are more likely to pay attention to stuff that is scary and threatening. Of course, learning about a lot of scary news also makes people anxious. With day after day of frightening stories, people can start to think the world is much more dangerous than it is.

Have you ever heard the term, "clickbait?" What if you were doing internet research for a school report and suddenly saw a popup that said, "Thirteen-year-old shares secret for making a million!" Would you be curious? Would you click on it?

Clickbait is designed to attract attention. Its fast presentation encourages clicking before your brain can caution, "Hold on a minute! That sounds too good to be true!"

When a person is identified in the news and accused of a crime, the impression can stick, even if the accusation is proven false. But journalists know exciting stories are more likely to be read, so crime stories are quick to be reported by some. Unfortunately, a later correction stating someone didn't do anything wrong isn't very exciting and may not be believed, even if reported. This is not only unfair, but can cause long term harm to an innocent person.

Being aware of how descriptions of people and events may be influenced in ways that make them more interesting (but less accurate) can keep you from accepting false messages.

Now You Know

- When people share experiences, they often change details to make a more interesting story. This can lead to passing along inaccurate information.

- Just understanding information results in believing and accepting it, at least for the moment. It takes effort to question the information and decide that it might not be true.

- Information that is repeated and becomes familiar is easier to accept as true.

Answers:

Bubble Wrap: plastic cushioning wrap that has air pockets

Crocs: plastic shoes

Q-tips: small sticks with a bit of a cotton ball at each end

Sharpie: permanent markers

Frisbee: a plastic disc used to play catch

Hula Hoop: plastic circle a person can spin around their hips (well...some can!)

Post-its: bits of paper that temporarily stick to other paper

Band-Aids: small bandages that can be stuck over cuts

Tupperware: plastic food containers

Zamboni: vehicles that smooth ice at an ice-rink

CHAPTER 4

How Does It Feel?

On Halloween morning in 1938, an alarming report came over the radio announcing a Martian invasion of New Jersey. At that time, there was no TV and no internet! The program called *War of the Worlds* was just entertainment, but people who tuned in late missed hearing that part. It sounded just like a news program!

Many people knew the story, that Martians had taken over the planet in less than 40 minutes, wasn't true. But some people became terrified. Their strong **emotions** clouded their judgement that the story didn't make sense. How did they become fooled by such a wild tale? What does it say about humans' ability to think clearly when frightened?

Emotion: the sense people make of, and the labels they use, to understand bodily sensations in a given situation.

Large machines are crushing buildings, everything is on fire. There's panic in the streets as people try to flee. I've never seen anything like this before!

Officials around the world are reporting similar occurrences. Our army has been deployed to stop this aggression from this unknown invader. Stay calm, people!

We're under attack! Creatures from outer space are here!

Getting Emotional

Coping with strong emotions causes yet another brain glitch. When we experience strong emotions, we have a hard time thinking clearly. We can even have trouble making good judgements about whether something is a real threat or not.

Take the example of the stink bug. Stink bugs are small brown bugs that were accidentally brought from Asia to the Mid-Atlantic U.S. in the 1990s. They probably hitched a ride in a shipping crate. Little stink bugs really liked the environment. They set up homes and began to have lots of baby stink bugs, usually as the weather warms in spring. Often, they hatch in houses and there can be a lot of them. Television reporters often cover their appearance in excited tones. All that attention gets people worked up, even afraid! Pretty soon some folks start freaking out after finding even one of these small brown invaders.

But stink bugs don't bite or cause any harm to humans. If there are enough of them, they can hurt plants, but so far, they haven't really been a problem for farmers. For most people the worst thing is a bad smell that happens if the bugs are squashed. So why all the fuss?

Stink bugs aren't the only critters folks worry about more than makes sense. Sometimes just their names can sound frightening. Read about:

- Dog-strangling vines
- Wolf spiders
- Murder hornets
- Death-head hawkmoths

Find out how they got their names and whether they are as scary as they sound.

Let's think a minute about emotions. How do fear, anxiety, joy, and other emotions come about? It turns out emotions have a lot to do with the context in which you find yourself and the cues that surround you about what an experience means. Let's say you are riding a roller coaster. As you climb up and then plunge downward, **adrenaline** pumps through your body. Your heart beats fast, you sweat, and you breathe quicker. This is FUN!

But your body's response to a roller coaster ride is a lot like the reaction you'd have if you were walking along a wooded trail and saw a bear in front of you. Adrenaline pumps through your body. Your heart starts to beat fast, you sweat, and you breathe rapidly. You get the same body signals, but this time you experience FEAR or even TERROR! What gives? The same feelings cause different emotions?

Emotion is determined not only by what you feel, but also by how you understand and label it. To understand what your feelings mean, you look for clues around you. Are you at an amusement park or in the wilderness? Are people nearby laughing and smiling when they scream, or do they have a panicked expression as they run away?

Adrenaline: a hormone that prepares your body for exertion by increasing breathing and blood flow.

CHECK OUT THE RESEARCH

The connection between your body's reactions and emotions can go both ways. How your body feels can also change what you think. This happens without you even being aware of it. Psychologists Jane Risen and Clayton Critcher asked two groups of people how seriously they worried about global warming. The only difference between the groups was that one was questioned in a very warm room and the other in a cold room.

Of course, the temperature of the rooms had nothing to do with the question. But the people in the warm room were more concerned about the warming planet than those in the cold room.

Can Behavior Change Beliefs?

Okay, ready to be really surprised? It also turns out that "what you do is what you think!" Your own behavior can change how you understand your feelings. Psychologist Daryl Bem developed a theory that when body signals aren't clear, the way we act can influence how we understand them. Kind of a kooky idea that's a bit confusing, but what he's saying is: If you quickly gobble down a big sandwich, it may convince you that you must have been really hungry.

CHECK OUT THE RESEARCH

Knowing that people's behavior can change what they think may make you wonder— can you change beliefs by getting someone to do something? Researchers Gary Wells and Richard Petty wondered that too. Their research tested whether people's gestures could change their opinions. Turns out people asked to nod their head "yes" while testing new headphones were more likely to rate the headphones as good quality than folks told to shake their head "no." Isn't that interesting?

In another study, John Cacioppo and team found that having people pull their hands towards themselves made them more likely to accept an idea than people told to push their hands away.

sounds great

YES

sounds bad

NO

Emotions High, Now What Do I Do?

When we sense danger, our bodies become worked up. We don't stop to think. We take action to protect ourselves. Reacting quickly and automatically in the face of danger is important for safety. If you hear a crash of thunder, you need to take cover from lightning. If you stopped to check the weather radar on a cell phone before heading indoors, you might be hurt!

Your brain needs to recognize danger quickly so you can act! This speed can be a lifesaver. But it leaves no time for careful thinking. Your emergency warning system can make you miss signs that all is well. You may end up feeling threatened even at times when you are perfectly safe.

Ever wonder what happens in your brain when scary things pop out of nowhere in a horror movie? It's the same as when someone sneaks up behind you and pounces! When you are startled in real life or when watching a film, your **amygdala** (the part of your brain that signals fear) jumps into action. It shoots a message to the **hypothalamus** (another part of your brain) to release adrenaline (a hormone) to prepare your body for fight or flight!

When we sense danger, our bodies get ready to fight off a threat or run from it. You may have heard of this "fight or flight response." This response also affects how we think and process information. Your emotions take over and instincts kick in. You switch to being on the lookout for other dangers and scanning around for threats. This is called **automatic vigilance**. Critical thinking shuts down. It all happens in a split second without you knowing! Then it's easy to believe messages that speak to our fears and skip over rational thoughts.

Amygdala: a part of the brain involved with anger, fear, and memory.

Hypothalamus: a part of your brain that regulates many bodily functions.

Automatic vigilance: an unconscious fear response that leads people to look for danger. It can sometimes lead us to perceive threats that aren't real.

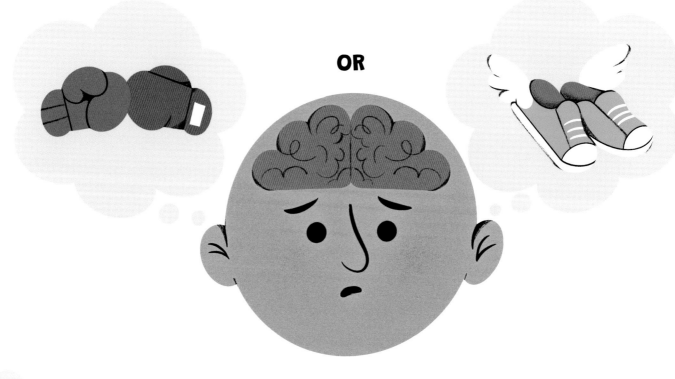

OR

DID YOU KNOW?

Positive experiences make us expect more positive experiences. But fear and anxiety are even more powerful in creating worry about threats and automatic vigilance.

Stress Can Change What You Think

Just like fear and anxiety, stress can change how and what we believe. When people are under stress, they see the world as more dangerous. Stressed people show more automatic vigilance and less critical thinking happens.

CHECK OUT THE RESEARCH

Neil Garret and colleagues wondered if stress made people worry more. They told one group of people (the experimental group) they would be giving a presentation to a group of strangers and their performance would be recorded. The researchers figured this would stress them out. Measures of the stress hormone, cortisol, showed it did. A second group of people (the control group) were told to plan a presentation, but they didn't have to give it. This no-stress group showed lower levels of cortisol.

Next, both groups rated how likely it was that something bad would happen to them in the future, like a car accident or a robbery. The high-stress/high-cortisol level experimental group was more likely than low-stress controls to think they'd face future bad experiences. When people are frightened or stressed, they feel more vulnerable and tend to be on the lookout for danger.

Increase belief in future bad experiences

Increased stress hormones

Presentation in front of others

When Emotions Rule Behavior

People hate losing. Research has shown they hate it even more than they like winning. In fact, people hate losing so much they'd give up some winning not to lose!

The way a choice is described can change how people decide how much risk to take. For example, Daniel Kahneman and Amos Tversky asked research participants to imagine a deadly disease outbreak, and then asked them to choose between two outcomes.

Outcome A	400 people will die
Outcome B	big chance that everyone will die but a small chance that no one will die

If you read both options closely, the numbers suggest that a large amount of people could die in either one. However, most people chose Outcome B. They felt uncomfortable with Outcome A because 400 people definitely would die. The idea of a sure loss was less acceptable than taking a chance on an outcome described in less definite way.

Try This

Suppose you were told that, based on a coin toss, you could either lose $10 or win $15. Would you accept the deal?

Most people wouldn't. But that makes no sense, since the prize for winning is higher than the cost of losing. Yet most people won't take the chance unless the reward for winning is two times more than the cost of losing.

Can You Scare People Into Better Behavior?

Believing something is the right thing to do isn't always enough to get people to take responsible action. But under some circumstances fear can be very effective at influencing both beliefs and behavior.

Psychologist Tali Sharot figured out that fear is very effective if you want someone to not do something. For example, if you tell someone the egg salad at a picnic has been sitting in the sun for too long and could cause food poisoning, they won't eat it. If you say your dog bites, few people will reach out to pet her.

But fear doesn't work as well if you want to get people to take action. In that case, **positive feedback** (information that what they're doing is the right thing), is a more successful strategy.

> **Positive feedback:** information indicating a behavior is working, making it more likely someone will do it again.

─ CHECK OUT THE RESEARCH ─

It's important that healthcare workers wash their hands frequently, so they don't spread diseases from one patient to another. This is well known by medical staff, but not always done. Donna Armellino and fellow researchers set up a video camera to check whether healthcare workers regularly washed their hands between visiting patients' rooms. The staff knew they were being watched, but only one person out of 10 took time to do a good wash. That was until the researchers set up a display board showing how well everyone was doing with handwashing. This positive feedback led to almost all the staff washing well between patient contacts.

> Fantastic! All that practice is paying off! You shaved off 5 seconds!

We often have stereotypes about people with disabilities. Sometimes that's true even for a person with a disability. Do you think a blind person could be a mountain climber? Erik Weihehmayer, who become blind as a teen, didn't think so. Then he learned about a rockclimbing class for blind kids. He signed up. He was good at it and the confidence he gained led him to challenge beliefs about what blind people could do. Erik went on to become a world-class climber, reaching the summits of mountains even sighted climbers find challenging. This included reaching the top of Mt. Everest. He founded a movement called, "No Barriers" to encourage people to take on challenges and push back on stereotypes about what they can and can't do.

Emotion and Prejudice

We know that upsetting emotions change how we think about things, but what about people? Could negative feelings towards groups of people influence our perceptions of them?

Stereotypes are assumptions and feelings we have about groups of people. While stereotypes may include positive feelings (like assuming someone who wears glasses is brainy) many are linked to negative feelings and beliefs. This can include negative feelings about minority groups and racism towards people of color.

Stereotypes: preconceived ideas about the typical preferences, beliefs, and behaviors of a group of people, and individuals within that group.

On September 11, 2001, terrorists attacked the United States. They destroyed a skyscraper (the World Trade Center) in New York, hit the Pentagon in Washington, and crashed a plane full of passengers in Pennsylvania. Thousands of Americans were killed, and the country was afraid there would be more attacks. The terrorists were identified as "Islamic extremists." Following this attack, Muslims (people whose religion is Islam) were seen as threats to their communities and sometimes mistreated. Can you see how stereotypes and automatic vigilance contributed to this unfair reaction?

Real World Impact

In a real crisis, police often have to quickly decide whether a person poses a threat. Based on what you've read about the research, perhaps it's not surprising that stereotypes can lead to deadly mistakes. People make assumptions about what a person may be holding or reaching for or what their intentions are. Such instances of people killing Black men have increased in recent years, but these events are not new. Our history is full of stories of people of color being incorrectly perceived as threatening, often with deadly results.

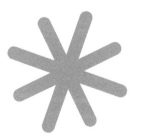

Try This

Sometimes people take advantage of emotional reactions to gain attention and influence others. How might heightening of emotions make it harder for listeners to think clearly and make accurate judgements about events in the news? Products we buy? Jury decisions?

Pay attention to this as you see ads on shows or YouTube. You might even see it happening in real life!

CHECK OUT THE RESEARCH

Psychologist B. Keith Payne wondered if stereotypes about race could lead to negative perceptions of people of color. Do stereotypes about Black men make people automatically see them as threatening even when they are not? Could automatic vigilance be a factor?

To explore this, Payne showed people either a Black person's face or a White person's face, quickly followed by a drawing of a gun or a hand tool. The presentations were very fast, and the person needed to make a split-second decision about what they had seen. Because it was hard to make decisions so fast, people made a lot of errors. But those errors were not random. When White people were judging, a hand tool was more often incorrectly seen as a gun if they had seen a Black face immediately before. The experiment seemed to show that when a White person saw a Black person's face the White person's automatic vigilance kicked in, and they were on the lookout for danger. They perceived a threat even when it wasn't there.

Now You Know

- Emotions result from our labeling of physical reactions to an event or experience.

- How we feel can influence our judgements and beliefs.

- Fear, anxiety, and stress can lead us to search for threats.

- Fear can be an effective way to stop someone from doing something but is less effective at convincing them to take action.

- Stereotypes that include negative feelings can interfere with clear thinking and lead to incorrect judgements about others.

CHAPTER 5

Does It Fit? ?

Your friend sits down next to you at lunch and tells you they've just learned an interesting fact: Snow can warm you up. You look carefully to see if there is any hint they're joking or setting you up. You search your brain to come up with an idea of how something cold could warm you. Could it have something to do with the burn you feel when you hold ice in your hand for too long?

Whatever your thoughts are, you won't just accept what they say without question. The idea of snow warming you does not fit your experience of snow or what you know about it from books, movies, or TV shows. The idea would probably make you feel confused and even uncomfortable as you try to figure out if this could be true. Is it some kind of trick? Are they making it up?

When we learn something new, we quickly run through what we already know. Does it seem familiar? Does it fit with our experiences? Does it fit with other things we think are true? It's a strategy that works most of the time. It helps us instantly ignore things that seem nonsensical. But it's a strategy that isn't foolproof, and at times can lead us to wrong conclusions.

In this case, your friend wasn't setting you up to look foolish, but was sharing a cool fact. Snow is made up mostly of trapped air. Just like in a puffy winter coat, that trapped air is great insulation. Animals who live in cold places burrow deep into the snow to keep warm in winter. It's also the reason igloos stay warm, by trapping warm air in a big bubble.

CHECK OUT THE RESEARCH

Our brains prefer to take it easy. Information that is easy to understand is easier to believe. Psychologist Daniel Kahneman has said that this can result in "truth illusions." Using simple words instead of complicated explanations, catchy words or phrases, and even a font that is easy to read can make a message more believable.

unostentatious lexicon conveys propositions less indisputably

Easy words make things believable

The Familiar Feels Safe

Everyone feels more comfortable with things that are familiar. Psychologist Robert Zajonc had a theory that this was because, to survive in a dangerous environment, humans needed to be very careful with things that were unusual. Things they already had experienced could be accepted as safe.

Try This

How willing are you to try new foods? Have you ever been at a restaurant or a friend's house and been served food you'd never seen or tasted before? Did you eat it without questions or hesitation? Which of these foods would you try?

- a raw, leafy green vegetable that looks like tree leaves
- a piece of fruit that looks like a yellow prickly cactus
- a veggie that smells like rotting meat
- a fried insect
- a small brown crab (with legs and shell) on a slice of bread
- a jellied slice with bits of meat
- the heart or intestines of a cow
- a guinea pig
- fried frogs' legs
- snails
- soup made from a snake
- cheese with blue moldy bits

Although all of these foods are eaten somewhere in the world, they may be unfamiliar (and weird) to you. Many people would refuse to eat them. But very young children often avoid foods that are healthy and nutritious (like vegetables), in part because they prefer food that is familiar. Even adults sometimes avoid foods simply because they've never tried them. There's even a label for this: food neophobia, meaning "fear of new food." It turns out being exposed to a new food can make it more acceptable, but only if that exposure includes tasting it. Why? Because exposure to something makes it more familiar!

It makes sense that people might be cautious about trying new foods. After all, our ancient ancestors might have been poisoned by eating an unknown plant or creature. So, that explains why we don't munch down on just any old thing, right?

Well, it could explain why we might not want to try new foods, but that's not the only unfamiliar thing humans are hesitant about. We even feel uncomfortable with unfamiliar words!

Try This

Have you ever felt frustrated when a word you don't know pops up in something you're reading? Might your reaction to a lot of unfamiliar vocabulary make you like a book less? (Okay, reader…maybe I owe you an apology!)

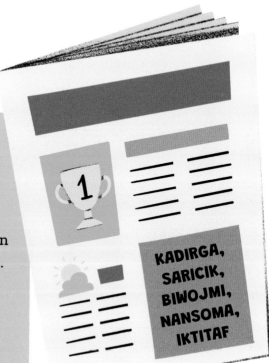

CHECK OUT THE RESEARCH

Drs. Zajonc and Rajecki were curious about whether people might prefer words that were familiar. To see, they put some Turkish words in an American college newspaper over and over again. They wanted students to see them as familiar (even if they didn't know what they meant).

Later, they asked students how they felt about these words compared to Turkish words they had not seen before. The students said they liked the now familiar words better.

Sticking With What You Know Is Easier

When we hear something that doesn't fit with what we know, it makes sense to question it. If I told you wheels don't roll, you would doubt me. After all, in your experience rolling is what wheels do best. Ignoring things that don't fit makes you efficient. Imagine how much time and brain power would be required if you had to figure out if every wheel you saw rolled!

Constantly questioning everything would be overwhelming. But there is a price we pay for this efficiency. Sometimes we instantly reject true information without carefully thinking it through.

When things don't fit, it takes extra time to make sense of them. This is called the Stroop Effect. One way it's demonstrated is with a test like this.
Read these words:

RED **BLUE** GREEN

Now, try these:

RED YELLOW **GREEN**

Of course, you can do it but if you go too fast you may make mistakes. Not sure you believe it? You can find the Stroop Test online. Can you go as fast when the colors and words don't match?

New Information Can Shake You up

Have you ever felt uncomfortable when a friend commented that a book or show you love is childish or "dumb?" Did it make you wonder if you should change your mind about it? Or maybe you felt great about how you studied for a test or performed in a sport, but had an adult seem disappointed and suggest perhaps you should work a bit harder next time. When new ideas clash with old ones it can be unsettling.

Information that doesn't fit can make us tense. When this happens, we search for ways to reduce that uncomfortable feeling. One option is to decide the new information isn't true. Or you might change how you understand what the new information means or what you thought before in order to fit them together. But if your old belief was just plain wrong, you run the risk of clinging tightly to something that isn't true.

I need to do more drills to up my skills.

Accepting new information

Athletes need to balance hard work and periods of rest.

Changing the meanings to fit old and new ideas together

I'm working just as hard as I can.

Rejecting new information

Psychologist Leon Festinger described this experience with a theory of what happens when old ideas conflict with new ones. When you learn something that fits what you already think, no problem. You accept it and move on. He called this **cognitive consistency**. If new information doesn't fit, it makes you uncomfortable and you experience **cognitive dissonance**. When that happens, you may reject the new information or explain it away. Of course, you can also change what you think. But dealing with cognitive dissonance takes mental effort. It can be uncomfortable and requires work. And if you haven't realized it yet, human brains like to take things easy.

Sometimes, your own actions can lead to a sense that things don't fit. When your behavior doesn't fit with how you think of yourself, you're left with conflicting self-views. For instance, if you think of yourself as an honest person but you tell a lie, that twinge you feel is cognitive dissonance.

Cognitive consistency: when two ideas fit together.

Cognitive dissonance: when ideas don't fit together. Sometimes this causes us to be uncomfortable.

If new information fits what we know, it's easy to accept it.

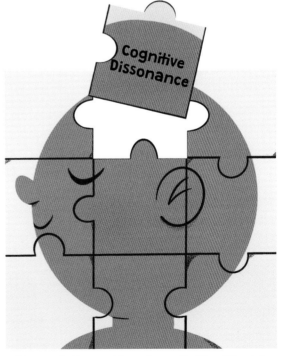

If new information doesn't fit with old ideas, we have to decide whether to change what we think or ignore it.

How Might You React?

Imagine you are walking your dog (imagine you have a dog if you don't already) and your dog does what dogs often do—poops! You've forgotten to bring a plastic bag. Your dog has chosen a spot on the sidewalk at a park where kids ride bikes and older people rest on benches under the trees. In fact, your dog's poop landed right under a sign reminding people to clean up after their pets.

If you've ever faced this real-life experiment, chances are you felt bad or embarrassed, or guilty. You may have checked around to be sure no one saw. In other words, you experienced cognitive dissonance. How might you deal with the conflict between seeing yourself as a responsible, thoughtful person and leaving that mess for someone to step in? What kinds of thoughts might help you deal with the discomfort you'd feel?

When our reasons for why we did something don't make sense, we may change those reasons. Sometimes this can lead to unexpected things. For example, you might be surprised to learn that something you enjoy may be less fun if you get paid for it! Hard to believe, but research by Dr. Festinger showed exactly this. And it's been proven again and again for over half a century since he did. What's going on here? Cognitive dissonance is causing you to rethink whether you're doing something you want to do or whether you're doing work.

I like helping to clean!

I hate chores!

VS.

Even little kids experience cognitive dissonance. In a study by Mark Lepper and others, preschoolers were given a treat of drawing with felt markers. Some were told they would get a prize for using the markers. Others got an unexpected prize after finishing their pictures. But a third group got no prize at all. Which group of kids enjoyed using the markers most? At this point you know enough to guess it was the last group. In their heads they had made the pictures for fun, not for a prize.

Accepting What Fits, Ignoring What Doesn't

The easiest thing to do when new facts lead to cognitive dissonance is just reject them. Why deal with all these squirmy feelings at all? Of course, the answer is if what gets thrown in the reject pile of ideas is actually true, it can be a problem. You might get stuck with old, wrong ideas and not benefit from new accurate ones.

CHECK OUT THE RESEARCH

Researcher C. Sunstein and colleagues shared facts about climate change with two groups of people. One group already believed in human-caused climate change. The second group did not. Both groups got the same evidence of changes in climate, some good and some bad. Both groups took bits of information that fit what they already thought. They ignored facts that did not fit what they already believed.

Sometimes a whole group of people shares ideas that aren't true. When this happens, those beliefs can be really hard to change. Clinging to ideas that don't seem sensible can be difficult for people outside of the group to understand.

In 1956, Dr. Festinger and others became aware of a group of people who believed the entire American continent would be flooded. They had gotten this idea from one person they saw as a prophet. She said she had received this information from outer space and that a flying saucer would come to save everyone who believed her story. The researchers wondered what would happen when there was no flood and no spaceship. How would people deal with their cognitive dissonance?

It turned out that group members who were alone when the predictions didn't happen changed their belief. They decided the prophecy wasn't true. But those who were with others from the group when the predictions didn't happen continued to believe the prophecy had been correct, even though there was no flood. Instead of seeing the lack of flood and spaceship as evidence that the woman wasn't really a prophet, they changed the story to fit the new evidence (so the new information fit the old belief). They decided the world had been saved because of their goodness. This actually strengthened their belief in the alien messages, and they began to share this message with others.

You'll continue to learn more about the impact of others on our beliefs in a later chapter.

Real World Impact

Many behaviors have been shown to influence our health and wellbeing. Doctors encourage people to make healthy changes to reduce their chances of disease. People who smoke are told how important it is to quit. Kids and adults who are obese are encouraged to exercise and make changes to their diets. But each of these recommendations is likely to cause cognitive dissonance. Rather than improving health-related behavior, advice to change longstanding familiar behaviors can sometimes backfire. Instead, people may think of all the reasons why this information does not apply to them.

Now You Know

- Messages that fit with ideas we already have are easier to accept. This makes us more efficient, but may make us reject new, accurate information.

- When new messages challenge what we have learned in the past, it creates tension. This is called cognitive dissonance.

- Cognitive dissonance can result in (correctly or incorrectly) explaining away or ignoring new information.

- Thinking new ideas through carefully takes work.

CHAPTER 6
Strengthening Our Beliefs

It's the depths of winter. Weather forecasters are calling for snow. They say it might be a big one. You sure could use a day off from school. Hope tomorrow will be a snow day! You know just what to do to make it come true. You text your friends, tell your siblings, and even ask your parents to help. "Everyone, wear your PJs inside out and backwards!" (If you live where there is no snow, let me assure you this is a thing for kids in colder places.)

The next day it's even snowier than predicted! SNOW DAY! Did the PJs do the trick? Did the wonky way you wore them give you a chance for sledding or building snowmen or lazing inside drinking cocoa? While you may not really think you can influence the weather, this superstition has managed to stick. Why?

The power of backwards PJs is not the only superstition. Have you ever been on a ghost tour? Lots of cities and towns have them. They usually happen after dark to add to the spooky feeling. Folks meet up with a guide who takes them to spots where something bad happened in the past or where people have reported strange experiences, things they think mean a ghost (or sometimes more than one) visits regularly. The idea of ghosts can be fun, but most people know they're not real. So, why would someone believe in them?

Some people pretend to believe in ghosts for fun. But others think they're real. Most of us wonder what happens after people die. Some believe their souls go to heaven, others that they are reincarnated (their souls reborn in another being). But for hundreds of years stories have been told about places where traumatic events happened, including tales about people who died staying around to haunt the living. Sometimes these ghosts were victims of violent crimes or people who are mad at the living. In some cases, stories include seeing, hearing, or getting secret messages from the dead. Later, others may add to the stories with similar experiences of their own. How do these stories grow? What would make someone believe they see or hear ghosts?

EXPLORE FURTHER

Are there ghost stories about places near you? A trip to your local public library can be one way to find out. Ask a librarian for help finding information about stories of ghosts or spooky places you might not know about.

Finding Evidence

When scientists or investigative journalists look for evidence about what is true and what is false, they are methodical in their approach.

They not only look for information that supports their hypothesis, but also information that contradicts it, or could prove it isn't true. But in our everyday lives we often look only for information that fits what we think. We don't look for information that could prove us wrong.

Confirmation bias: the tendency for people to seek out information that supports the views they already have.

One explanation for people's belief in ghosts and hauntings (and the power of backwards PJs) is called **confirmation bias**. If a person thinks something is true, they look for evidence that fits with that idea and ignore things that don't. They don't do it on purpose. In fact, they don't even know that's what they are doing.

What are other words for methodical?

Systematic, orderly, regular, organized, business like, neat, precise, meticulous, structured, ordered.

Look at this set of numbers. What three numbers do you think come next? Do you see a pattern?

2, 4, 6, _, _, _
3, 5, 7, _, _, _
10, 12, 14, _, _, _

What rule did you use to answer this problem? Did you think it's "add 2?" Most people do. Now test your rule on this set of numbers:

6, 8, 10, _, _, _
15, 17, 19, _, _, _
21, 23, 25, _, _, _

What if you were told that these numbers also would work and fit the pattern:

7, 8, 10
9, 11, 15
18, 20, 25

But they don't fit the "add 2" rule! It turns out there is another rule that works. Instead of adding two to each number, the next number had to be bigger than the one before it! Tricky, right?

This is exactly the problem that psychologist Peter Wason used in his research. He found that most people stick to their first guess and don't consider possibilities that could prove it wrong.

Research participants had found a rule to fit the first example, but then only looked for information that proved they were right.

They didn't test other series of numbers that would have proved their first guess was wrong. Did you make the same mistake? If so, no worries. It just means you sometimes make mistakes due to confirmation bias, just like the rest of us!

Failing To Look for Alternatives

Let's go back to those haunted houses. If Casey and Jess believe in haunted houses, they may tell each other stories about people who say they've experienced a haunted place. They may search the internet to see if anyone else saw or heard something similar at that place. Or they may try to find more details about what scary things happened there in the past. The more they learn about hauntings, the more exciting it may seem.

They might even decide to check out an old house in town that's supposed to have a ghost of its own. If they did, chances are they would notice details that fit with their expectations of a haunted house. They might hear an unusual noise and tell each other it's a ghost moaning. They might feel movement across their cheeks and think a ghost had passed close by, even though no one was there.

As Casey and Jess search for signs of a haunting, they might not think about other possible causes of those signs, not to mention the perfectly normal things that occur. They may miss the fact that wind is causing drafts through broken windows. Or that the wind is moving the branches of a tree outside, creating a weird creaking noise. And the fact that nothing bad happened to them while poking around and gathering evidence of threatening spirits would probably not grab their attention at all. When Casey and Jess search for (and find) signs of a haunted house without considering other causes of the signs, they are experiencing confirmation bias.

GHOSTS	NO GHOSTS
moaning noises	wind blowing through broken windows
creaking noises	tree limbs bending
something touching my cheek	draft on my face
feeling scared	nothing bad happened to me

What's the Question?

Sometimes the way a question is worded can also lead to confirmation bias. Consider the following study.

Researcher Jennifer Crocker asked two groups of people to figure out if a hard workout the day before a tennis match was a winning strategy. Participants were then told how players had done after a workout, compared to how they had performed after a day of rest.

But the two groups were asked using slightly different words. The first group was asked if a hard workout before a match led to more wins. The second group was asked if a hard workout before a match led to more losses. While these questions seem basically the same, the type of information the groups looked for was different. The first group only looked at wins. The second group only considered losses. Even though participants had no reason to prefer one outcome over another, they only looked for information that could confirm the question they were trying to answer.

Try This

What if your friend said, "Dogs are much better pets than cats." If you love your cat, you might want to prove how wrong they are. Try an internet search to see if you can find evidence. Type in "cats are better than dogs." You will probably find quite a few advantages cats have over dogs. So cats make better pets, right?

Turns out your search led you down the confirmation bias path. What happens if you look for evidence to disprove your statement? Try searching, "dogs are better than cats." Can you see how only searching for things that prove your idea might lead to a biased conclusion?

Confirming Wrong Ideas About People

While the idea of ghosts and haunted houses is kind of fun and rarely leads to problems, confirmation bias can be hurtful. Confirmation bias contributes to many kinds of negative stereotypes that can result in inaccurate and unfair judgements of others. If we think a group of people has certain characteristics, we tend to notice evidence that fits the stereotype and ignore evidence that doesn't fit.

For instance, if we think boys are athletic and girls prefer books, we may notice when Eli makes a great soccer goal and miss when Sasha scores a tough basketball shot. And we may take note when Sasha is reading during recess, but not pay attention to the huge stack of books Eli checks out of the library.

Stereotypes can influence us even without our being aware of it. This is called **implicit bias**. In fact, this bias can continue to influence our perceptions even if, rationally and consciously, we think they are wrong.

Implicit bias: an unconscious negative reaction to (or preference for) a person or a group.

Implicit Bias at Work

Look at this list of characteristics. Do you automatically group some things with others? If so, you're not alone. People make unfair and inaccurate judgments all the time. This is implicit bias at work.

Big Latino/a Nerdy Quiet
Hyper **Small** **Tall**
Thin Athletic
Salsa Asian Old
Black Female Hispanic
Kind **Calm** Male
Helpful Loud Musical
Hip-hop
white Angry Fat FOOTBALL
Running **Smart** Boxing
Bossy GAMER
Young
Basketball Ballet **Short**

He's so tall! I'm sure he's great at basketball!

Thinking So Might Make It So

Stereotypes and implicit bias can result in false assumptions about people based on their race, gender identity, physical disability, accent, and which neighborhood they live in. They can also result in **self-fulfilling prophecies**. People may start believing what others are saying (or thinking) and just accept harmful or hateful stereotypes about them as true without even realizing it. Bias can lead to different expectations and opportunities for members of a group. The people within the group may even begin to see themselves as having those traits and not even try to achieve goals they may see as not meant for them.

Self-fulfilling prophecy: when you believe others' false ideas about you or your skills and change your behavior to fit their expectations.

For example, in the past many people believed girls were not as good as boys in math and science. As a result, teachers didn't encourage girls to take advanced science and math classes in high school. Girls, themselves, tended to lose interest in those subjects after elementary school because they worried they wouldn't do well in them.

Although women make up over half of the population of the United States, they have fewer (often far fewer) than half of the math and science related jobs.

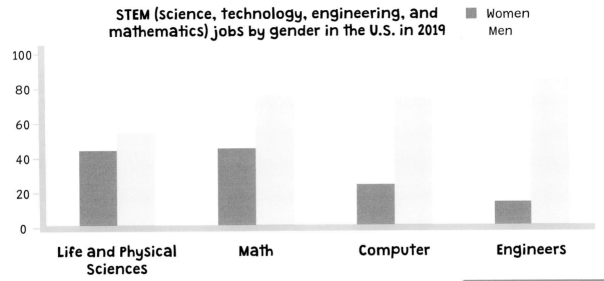

STEM (science, technology, engineering, and mathematics) jobs by gender in the U.S. in 2019 — Women / Men

CHECK OUT THE RESEARCH

Beliefs about kids' abilities can have a big impact on their school performance. Researchers Robert Rosenthal and Eleanor Jacobson wondered if beliefs about abilities might actually change or influence those abilities. They gave teachers a list of students, all identified as very smart. Actually, those students had been picked randomly. There was no reason to think they were smarter than their classmates. But when the class was given intelligence tests at the end of the year, kids previously labeled as smart actually had higher **IQs** than their classmates. This was shocking since, unlike grades and learned knowledge, intelligence (or your innate smarts) isn't something we think changes much over time. Teachers also reported kids in the "smart" group (who really weren't any smarter) were more curious, happier, and independent.

Just being told that some of their students were smart created a bias in teachers. Not only did they think of the kids as better learners, but those students also were perceived as having lots of other good qualities, too. Being regarded in a constant positive way by their teachers actually made the kids score higher on intelligence tests.

IQ: standing for "Intelligence Quotient," this measurement is based on a set of tests designed to measure how well someone can think and learn.

Try This

Do some research to learn about people who pushed back against the expectations of other people and succeeded where they were expected to fail.
Here's a list to get you started:

- Helen Keller
- Frederick Douglass
- Marie Curie
- Ludwig van Beethoven
- Stephen Hawking

Stereotypes can lead to differences in how much teachers encourage students and offer them opportunities. When this happens, it's not surprising that some kids will work hard to do well, while others may see themselves as less able to succeed. This is what seemed to happen in the Rosenthal and Jacobson study. When different teaching behaviors lead to the exact results that were predicted, the predictions appear to have been true (the definition of a self-fulfilling prophecy!).

When a prediction about someone's abilities fails to come true, it works against confirmation bias. But it can be a struggle for the person involved. Do you think the unexpected success of these individuals changed others' beliefs about them? Do you think these kinds of success stories can change implicit bias about others who share the same challenges?

Try This

Imagine you've just moved to a new school. The teacher puts you on the spot by making you "team captain" for Game Day. Your first assignment is to pick your six-member team. You have no idea what kind of games are involved.

Who would you choose? Would your choices be different if you learned the games involved mental puzzles? Athletic contests? Charades? How did you choose your team? Examine your choices. What assumptions did you make about each of the kids? Do you think implicit bias influenced your decisions?

Implicit bias can have an even greater impact on us when we are with strangers. While it can be uncomfortable to accept, we all have implicit biases. Understanding this and challenging our assumptions about other people is one way we can try to overcome them.

Real World Impact

Confirmation bias can make it hard for stereotypes to be corrected by later experiences. When incorrect ideas include negative views of entire groups of people it can lead to racism, antisemitism, anti-LGBTQ attitudes, hatred, and other forms of discrimination. Stereotypes and implicit bias can also limit opportunities for those who use wheelchairs to get around, are blind, deaf, or older, and may set unfair obstacles in the way of achieving goals or making preferred life choices.

Now You Know

- The way we search for information can reinforce ideas we already believe (whether or not they are accurate).

- Negative stereotypes about groups of people can influence their opportunities and behavior.

- Implicit bias operates outside of our awareness.

CHAPTER 7

What Does Everyone Else Think?

If someone asked where you usually sit at lunch, you'd probably be able to answer easily. Chances are the answer has more to do with WHO you sit with than whether you sit near the front or the back of the lunchroom. Most kids sit with the same group of friends most of the time. And that friendship group is important.

Belonging to a group matters outside of school, too. The people in your family, the people you hang out with, the sports teams you play on, and folks in your neighborhood and town are special to you. Not just because you like them (you may not like them all). They're special because part of your **identity** (how you see yourself) comes from which groups you belong to. The importance of being connected in social groups is built into us!

> **Identity:** how a person sees themself, including where they fit in with others, their social roles, and their relationships.

Humans Are Social Animals

All this joining of groups started early. Ancient humans joined together for protection and to help each other find food and other necessities. The desire to belong to a group is part of who we are, and as basic to our functioning as food and water. Because of this strong drive to be part of a group, we work hard to get into groups and stay there. We don't want to lose those connections. That means being tuned in to what others in the group expect and being careful not to do anything that would get us pushed out. This creates social pressure to fit in. You know… peer pressure! Kids are not the only ones who experience it. Adults also have a strong need to fit in. In fact, pressure to be accepted by others is there even when others in the group aren't!

Oh, yeah, yeah, polka dots are cool! My mom made me wear this dumb thing!

CHECK OUT THE RESEARCH

People can feel social pressure even when no one else is around. A reminder that others could be watching is enough to influence behavior. Melissa Bateson, Daniel Nettle, and Gilbert Roberts found that people were more honest about paying for self-serve drinks in front of a poster with eyes "watching" them. When posters with flowers faced them, folks were more likely to skip out without paying. Eyes watching from a poster also reduced the amount of litter people left behind in a café, especially when the café was empty (and lacking the eyes of other patrons).

HONOR SYSTEM

We feel most at ease when our beliefs match those of other people in our social group. When people disagree, it causes tension. To ensure that everyone gets along, we are more likely to accept messages from people in our group than from outsiders, even if our group is wrong. If the topic is one that really matters to the group, those who question in-group ideas may worry about being criticized or even pushed out. All this can make clear thinking challenging.

Teaching, Learning, Sharing

Okay, so humans are social creatures and that was important thousands of years ago, and social pressure has advantages now. What else do we get from being social?

Well, what if you were on your own, say on a desert island, and only able to learn from your own personal experiences? Think of all the things you'd never know! You'd have to figure out how to get food and shelter and you'd never know the guy on the next island over already had a clever method to fish. In fact, you might not even know there was another island out there!

One of the big pluses of being connected to other people is the ability to learn from them. From the early teachings of parents to what you have learned from teachers, friends, books, and the internet, much of what you know came from others.

It's great that we can learn so easily from others. It helps us increase knowledge quickly and easily. We benefit from their experiences and knowledge, even those far distant from us in space and time. Discovering all of the planets revolving around our sun took hundreds of years. But you probably learned about them in kindergarten (or even before) simply by opening a book.

Try This

We sometimes think of peer pressure as bad. Of course, pressure to do something you shouldn't or that's dangerous isn't helpful, but often peer pressure is good. In fact, parents often encourage kids to follow their peers. Can you think of examples? Here are a few to get you started:

- A parent encourages a young child to share their toys.
- A kid pushes his friends to join him in reducing energy usage.
- Fans cheer on their team to score that goal!

The Challenge of Hand-Me-Down Information

You learned in Chapter 3 that when information passes from person to person it changes. As it moves through many people the original message may be very different from the original one. Some truth may be lost, and some false information may creep in. Because of this, secondhand knowledge may contain errors.

Try This

Have you ever played the game, "telephone?" If so, you've probably seen how information changes as it's passed from person to person. If the chain of people is long, the final message may be very different from the original one.

Gather some friends (the more, the better) for this experiment. Try a game of telephone. Have everyone get in a line. One person starts by whispering to the person next to them, "Information passed along rarely stays the same. Often details change." Then that person whispers it quietly to the next person, who then does the same to the next person, and so on. The last person in line says the message out loud. What message comes out last? How has it changed?

While our ability to learn from others is a great advantage, it also leaves us open to errors others make (and repeat), and to distortions of knowledge that have passed through many others. Whether it's someone close to us or someone we don't know at all, these sources of new information can, at times, be faulty and lead us to accept things that are not true.

What Do You Expect?

When people don't know what behavior is acceptable or expected in a social situation, they look at what others are doing. Other people's behavior provides clues about **social norms** (what is normal and acceptable behavior). Social norms can change from group to group, from situation to situation, and from time to time.

> **Social norms:** the informal rules of accepted behavior, attitudes, and beliefs of a culture or social group.

SOCIAL NORMS

Wait your turn

Cover your mouth when you cough

Raise your hand to speak

Don't bully

Brush your teeth

Offer assistance to people with disabilities

Don't gossip

Don't hurt others

Try This

While following some social norms can have serious consequences (like stopping for a red light), others may serve as a signal that someone is part of the group and "gets" its rules. Consider jeans. What style of jeans is in this year? What jeans would make a kid look clueless? Why are some jeans called "Mom jeans" or "Dad jeans?" Why do we even care about fashion?

Fashion, pop culture, and fads are all the result of a basic human need to fit in with others. They can provide clues to the group a person identifies with.

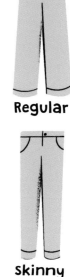

Regular

skinny

wide leg

boot cut

CHECK OUT THE RESEARCH

Have you heard of **code switching**? The term was first used to describe someone switching from speaking one language to another, depending on the listener. Later, it was used to describe how people from one social group changed styles of talking and slang to fit in with another group. More recently, code switching is used to describe when someone switches other outward signs of identity and culture, like self-expression, appearance, and behavior. Some Black people say that for them, code switching is necessary to thrive in workplaces or school, or simply to survive and keep safe in a world of traditionally White-dominated spaces.

Code switching: the name for changing your language, manner, or outward appearance depending on the social context and group you're in.

Even beyond norms, we often look to others when we lack information or feel confused. We may rely on the judgements, thoughts, and actions of other people to make sense of things. We're most likely to believe what members of a group we identify with think. All this looking at others to guide our behavior leads humans to be quick to accept what others think, do, and like, otherwise known as **conformity**.

Think about your favorite color. You probably think color preference is just a personal choice. But color popularity is influenced by other people, and changes over time. Do a quick computer search of popular decorator colors of the past. In the 1960s kitchens often had avocado green or harvest gold ovens and refrigerators. In the 1980s colors were bright pink, turquoise, and neon green. In the 2010s grey, tan, and white were favorite choices.

Why do people develop similar tastes at the same time? Even very personal preferences, like a favorite color, can be subject to the opinions of others.

Arthur Jenness explored conformity in the lab. He asked people to guess the number of beans in a jar. First, everyone had to make individual guesses. Some guessed too many, some guessed too few.

Then they were put in a room together and asked to talk about their guesses and decide on a group answer. Afterward, people were asked if they thought their own guess or the group guess was closer to the correct number. Almost everyone said the group guess was closer. They conformed to the group judgement.

> **Conformity:** the tendency to change behavior and/or beliefs to fit in with a social group.

EXPLORE FURTHER

Do you remember the Dr. Seuss story *Sneetches*? Look it up for a great example of conformity and trying to fit in with a group. Can you think of other examples in books, movies, or other types of entertainment?

Judging the number of beans in a jar can be hard to do. It might make sense to rely on other people's opinion in a situation where you don't feel confident about your own judgement. Especially when you know conforming to the ideas and behavior of a group can encourage positive outcomes. But conforming to the group can happen even at times when it seems like a bad idea. And research has shown that people sometimes go along with other people's judgement even when it's obviously wrong.

We're herd animals. In an emergency someone needs to say that we're heading towards the cliff. And everyone is just following, saying like, "Well, no one else is turning around, so I won't either." That could be very dangerous.

Greta Thunberg

– CHECK OUT THE RESEARCH –

Solomon Asch showed people two cards. One had a single line. The other had three lines, one of which matched the line on the first card.

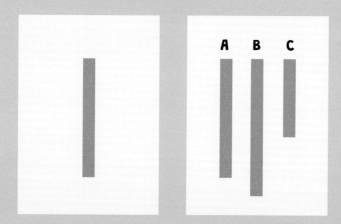

Next, he asked which line on the second card matched the one on the first card. Seems easy, right? But if people were in a group with an actor who made an incorrect choice, one out of three people agreed with that wrong answer!

CHECK OUT THE RESEARCH

What could make you eat something you don't like? Could it be as simple as knowing other people like it? Neuropsychologist Caroline Charpentier and colleagues had people come to their lab after fasting (these folks were hungry!). They asked them to rate how much they liked or disliked 80 different foods. Next, they were told what foods other people had chosen to eat at the end of the study and asked to make their own choices. Not only did hearing what other people wanted to eat influence people's choices, but they also chose to eat some foods they had said they disliked!

But there's more! These researchers were neuropsychologists. They were interested in what happens in brains. When people in their study learned other participants liked things they didn't, their brains reacted. Their brain function also registered when they had to choose between their own favorite or be influenced by other people's preferences. How cool is that!

Everybody Thinks So

Are you a sun worshiper? What if you invited a friend to join your family at the beach and they said, "No way! I'm staying in the AC all summer!" Sometimes, we can be surprised when people dislike something we like or when they see the world differently than we do. When we believe something, we assume most people agree with us. When this assumption is wrong, it's called the **false consensus effect**. Research shows people tend to think everyone shares their beliefs and think different opinions are far less popular.

> **False consensus effect:** the tendency to overestimate how many other people share our beliefs.

When Social Pressure Changes History

We tend to think of history as factual, but just like other stories passed down over time historical "facts" can begin to stray from truth. When newly discovered facts challenge traditional stories of the past it can feel threatening.

In the summer of 2021, a book talk at a history museum in Texas was called off within hours of its scheduled time. The governor and other state leaders on the museum's board insisted the event be canceled. The topic was the history of the Alamo. Why were these Texans worried about the talk? The book presented facts about a famous battle that had taken place in Texas in 1836. The story of that battle had become a heroic American myth (with some tweaking of the truth). In fact, the long-accepted understanding of the battle hid much of its real background. Like the fact that the battle had grown out of the desire to maintain slavery in the region. The more factual understanding of the story threatened the long-held view that participants in the battle had been heroes.

During the same year, some people in the country felt information about how unfair laws had affected Black people throughout the history of the United States did not belong in schools. But others in the country felt it was important to tell a more complete and realistic history of our nation.

Real World Impact

A kid is wound up and acting wild! Someone says, "Wow! That sugar sure hyped them up!" Many people have this idea that sugar makes kids "hyper," even though research has shown that's not true.

Where did this idea come from? In the 1970s Dr. Ben Feingold came up with a diet (the Feingold Diet) designed to treat kids with ADHD (Attention Deficit Hyperactivity Disorder). Dr. Feingold thought ADHD was due to food allergies and his diet suggested parents avoid food additives he thought were the cause. Sugar wasn't even on his list. But lots of stuff young kids eat has sugar in it. That got parents wondering and talking. Soon a full-fledged myth had developed.

Lots of medical studies followed to see if there was truth to the myth. In 1995, a report in one of the most important medical journals reviewed the best of these studies and concluded there was *no evidence* that sugar made kids more active. *1995!* And yet, many parents (and grandparents, and teachers, and even some doctors) still talk about how sugar makes kids "hyper."

Feeling pressure to go along with others is normal. Being aware of this pressure can help you stop and think things through, rather than simply going along with what others say or do.

They must have gotten into the candy!

Now You Know

- Humans evolved to be part of a social community for safety and efficiency. We rely on others to help us understand the world and how to function in it.

- Our strong motivation to fit into social groups results in pressure to conform to others' beliefs and expectations.

- We tend to overestimate how many others agree with our views.

- While making us more efficient, social pressure can result in errors in thinking and judgement.

PART TWO

Evidence and Errors:

The Science of Misinformation and Disinformation

So far, you've learned that human brains are amazing, but glitchy. The way our brains process information can lead to errors in perception and judgement. You also learned that the way information is presented can affect whether a message seems convincing, depending on who presents the information, and who else believes it is important. Sometimes these factors can lead to wrong beliefs about what is true and what is false.

Psychologists and others have used science to study this. But sometimes, misunderstanding how science works can be a problem too. In the next chapters, you will learn more about science methods. You'll also learn how misinformation and disinformation come about and are spread. Sometimes it happens by misunderstanding scientific findings. Errors can be shared widely from person to person, or by the media. Sometimes errors are shared by people who really think they are true. Other times, people twist facts on purpose. Armed with all this social psychological information, you will be better able to recognize when facts are being twisted.

CHAPTER 8

This Thing Called Science

When people eat more ice cream, the rate of shark attacks increases. This means eating frosty treats causes shark attacks!

How does that make sense?!?

It's not likely you would jump to such a weird conclusion, but leaps of logic like this happen more often than you'd think! It's hard to come up with a connection between sharks and ice cream. But when things we think could be related happen close together in time, it's easy to jump to the conclusion that one caused the other. Even in cases where it may "make sense," these mental leaps can lead to false conclusions. Why do we make these kinds of mistakes? How can we avoid them?

Our Wonderful Pattern Finding Abilities

Humans are great at finding patterns. This ability is built into our brains and helps us out a lot. Imagine trying to memorize a string of 12 random numbers.

5, 3, 8, 9, 11, 29, 17, 1, 44, 10, 37, 9

Now think how much easier it would be to remember 12 even numbers in order, beginning with two.

2, 4, 6, 8, 10, 12, 14, 16, 18, 20, 22, 24

Once you can identify a pattern, this memory task becomes easy. Patterns also help you predict the future. Consider the example below. What number comes next?

10, 20, 20, 40, __

Our skill at seeing patterns helps in ways that are more important than guessing the next number in a sequence. Math, physics, and computer science depend on seeing and using patterns. Engineers study patterns of car, bicycle, and pedestrian traffic to design signage and stoplights that improve safety. Babies learn language by recognizing patterns in the noises made by people around them. Patterns in songs and music are pleasant and help us build relationships with others who are able to sing along.

Try This

Think back to when you were very small. What songs or nursery rhymes can you still easily recall? Were there patterns that helped you learn them? Patterns such as:

- similar sounds, like rhymes
- repeating phrases, like the chorus of a song
- rhythms that are repeated
- melodies that are repeated

Patterns help us predict what might come next and make it easier to learn and remember.

Being good at quickly identifying patterns is a strength. Psychologists have found that intelligence and critical thinking are linked to strong pattern finding abilities.

Identifying Patterns Where They Are...and Aren't

Because patterns are so useful, we look for them. But in our searching, we sometimes see patterns even where none really exist. Perhaps you've heard of the "man in the moon." When we stare at a full moon, its craters can look like a human face. Or maybe you've looked at clouds and seen an object or an animal? Or maybe you started to recognize meaningful shapes in the cracks on a wall or sidewalk while bored. This happens to everyone and even has a name: **pareidolia**.

Pareidolia: the tendency to see recognizable objects or patterns in random visual displays.

There's a cow.

I see an airplane.

In addition to being alert to patterns in what we see and in numbers, we often see patterns in events around us. We do so even when those patterns aren't really there. This is called **apophenia**.

Our pattern radar helps us understand experiences and think about them in an organized way. It also helps us make educated guesses about what to expect in the future. But our preference for patterns can also mess us up! As in the case of ice cream and shark bites, it can lead us to leap to wrong conclusions. These leaps can become a problem when understanding science. It's easy for some types of scientific studies to be misunderstood. Let's take a look at **surveys**. Surveys typically include a bunch of questions in which people are asked about what they think or how they act.

> **Apophenia:** perceiving patterns or meaning in meaningless data.

> **Survey:** a list of questions aimed at gaining information about a particular topic.

It always rains on Saturday!

A Quick Survey of Survey Methods

Let's say you wanted to know what people think about life on other planets. This would be a great place to use a survey! They can be paper and pencil questionnaires, online tests, or interviews done in person or over the phone. If you were a psychologist, you might conduct a survey that asks a bunch of questions about alien life.

Do you think:

Yes No

- ☐ ☐ Life exists on other planets?
- ☐ ☐ Life-forms on other planets are the size of bacteria?
- ☐ ☐ Life-forms on other planets can move around on their own?
- ☐ ☐ Life-forms on other planets can think?
- ☐ ☐ Beings from other planets are aware of life on Earth?
- ☐ ☐ Beings from other planets have traveled to Earth?
- ☐ ☐ Humans have entered spaceships brought to Earth by aliens?
- ☐ ☐ Beings from other planets regularly observe humans?

Of course, you couldn't give your questionnaire to everyone on Earth, everyone in your country, or even everyone in your town. How would you choose who to have answer your questions?

One of the first decisions when doing a survey is who to survey. What **sample** of people will you ask to complete it? It's important that your sample is **representative** of all those you wish to learn about. In this example, it could be all people in America. So, if you were interested in what folks in the USA believed about aliens, you'd want to include all the different groups of people in the same percentages that make up the entire **population** of the United States, not just certain groups of people. You'd want to include people from different jobs, regions of the country, incomes, amount of schooling as well as ages, race, gender, and cultural background. It's not representative when you just ask one group and assume that their responses reflect what everyone would think! Phew! This is more complicated than it seemed!

Sample: the group of people who participate in a survey or research experiment.

Representative sample: a sample from a larger group that accurately mirrors the larger population of interest.

Population: in a research study, the larger community group the researcher is trying to learn about.

Try This

Imagine you heard that one of the math teachers in your school was much harder than another and you want to find out if it's true. You decide to test it with a survey.

- What kind of questions would you include?
- Who would you give your survey to?

Once you got your results, do you think you might have any hunches on what makes one teacher seem harder than another?

Does One Thing Lead to Another?

Surveys can be super helpful, but they have their limits. Think about this: A number of surveys have reported teens who eat dinner with their families most of the time are less likely to abuse drugs. Amazing! Could this be a way to stop drug abuse?

Perhaps, but wait a minute! Couldn't it be the other way around? Maybe kids who abuse drugs avoid family time. Or maybe a family problem makes it hard to have family meals and kids abuse drugs to escape tension in the family. We can't really say. The data from surveys are **correlations**. A correlation is a finding that two things often happen together. In the above example, eating dinner with the family and avoiding drugs were observed in the same teens. But it's a leap of logic to make a conclusion of **causation** (that either one made the other happen).

Correlation: when two things tend to change together, although it's not clear if one causes the other or if they are both changed by something else.

Causation: when one thing results in another thing happening.

Remember, just because one thing happens after another doesn't mean the first thing made the second happen. It could just be a coincidence that the two events happened close in time. Or a totally different thing could have made both happen. This doesn't mean research can't explore questions of causation. It just means a researcher may need to use a different method. They may need an **experiment** to explore further.

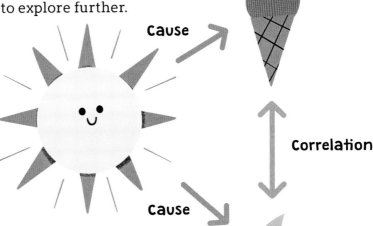

Experiment: a scientific test of a hypothesis.

Cause

Correlation

Cause

Try This

If someone advertised doing jumping jacks made kids between the ages of 9 and 10 grow, you'd probably realize most kids are growing at that age whether they do jumping jacks or not. But such false claims aren't always so easy to spot.

How might a diet food be falsely marketed as effective for people trying to control their weight? What other things might they be doing to lose weight that have nothing to do with that product?

Confusing correlation and causation is one way in which science is often misunderstood. By knowing the difference, you'll be better able to catch these errors. Is someone talking about causation when all that's known is that two things happen together?

The Scientific Method

This is called the **scientific method**. Surveys and other correlational data can help a researcher come up with guesses, or **hypotheses**, about what causes what. But a hypothesis is just the first step. Experiments test out whether or not things that seem to affect one another actually do.

Scientific method: using systematic observation, measurement, and experimentation to form and test hypotheses.

Hypothesis: an idea or possible explanation for something that has been observed and is tested through experimentation.

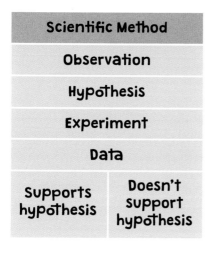

Scientific Method	
Observation	
Hypothesis	
Experiment	
Data	
Supports hypothesis	Doesn't support hypothesis

Control group  **compare** **Experimental group**

Expected results

Experimental results

The diference between the two: Evidence that is used to defend claims!

Experimental group: research participants who are subjected to an experimental procedure to test a hypothesis.

One kind of experiment compares two groups of people: one who experiences something (**experimental group**) and one who doesn't (**control group**).

To test their hypothesis, a psychologist might present a new situation or experience to people in an experiment. For example, what if you wanted to test whether an ad for a new video game called Zuzzle World would make kids want it? You choose a group of kids, being careful to have all kinds of kids in your sample (experiments need to use representative samples just like surveys). Next, you show them the advertisement and ask how many of them would ask for Zuzzle World.

Control group: research participants who are similar to people in the experimental group, but do not get the experimental treatment.

But what if it wasn't your ad that made Zuzzle World seem fun? What if the kids would want it even if they hadn't seen your convincing ad? If you had designed a good research study, you would have included a control group. Remember, a control group is another group of people who don't have the experimental experience. You need to know what would happen if they didn't see the ad. Then you would compare the data from your experimental group with the data from your control group. Do more kids who saw the ad want Zuzzle World? Or do kids want Zuzzle World even if they don't see your ad?

ZUZZLE WORLD

The best fun under the sun!

Of course, real experiments are a lot more complicated. If a psychologist were to do this study, they'd want to be sure the kids in both the experimental and control groups were similar. All the kids and their parents would also need to know they were participating in an experiment (secret experiments on people are not okay).

⎯ CHECK OUT THE RESEARCH ⎯

Not all research happens in a lab. A study that takes place in the real world is called a field experiment. A car maker in Sweden (Volkswagen) hypothesized that people would be encouraged to exercise for fun. They did their experiment on a flight of stairs next to an escalator. They watched how many people used the stairs (these people were the controls). Then, in the middle of the night, they changed the stairs into a piano keyboard that played notes when walked on (the experimental procedure). Next, they again observed and found that 66% more people now took stairs rather than an escalator.

EXPLORE FURTHER

You can find a video of the musical stairs by searching for "The Fun Theory: Piano Staircase"

One Is Never Enough

Once a survey or an experiment is finished, there's still more to do. Even the best designed study can't eliminate all types of errors. And sometimes the conclusions don't apply to all situations. This is where **replication** comes in. When a psychologist completes their research, they share the results with other researchers. They include details about the people who participated in the study and what they asked them or the experiences they presented to them.

> **Replication:** repeating a research study another scientist did to see if the same results happen.

Other psychologists repeat the study to see if they get the same results. Or a scientist does a study to test the same hypothesis in a different way. Conclusions can change as more research comes up with similar or different findings.

So, findings from one study aren't taken as the final word. Even before results are shared, research is evaluated by other scientists. Through this **peer review** other researchers (peers) check to see if careful methods were used and if the scientists' conclusions fit the data (review). Then, other scientists repeat the study to see if they come up with the same results—kind of like checking their work! Sometimes new studies use different approaches to test whether findings are the same, just to be sure.

> **Peer review:** when research is evaluated by other professionals with expertise in a given field. For scientific research, this includes deciding if proper research methods were used and if conclusions are consistent with reported data.

Understanding the human mind and behavior requires careful thought and planning. All of this checking and rechecking can take time. And it can be confusing when you hear the results of a study and later learn that further research found something different. In a later chapter you will read about how failure to understand how science works can lead to misunderstanding.

Now You Know

- When trying to answer questions about how people act or think, psychologists sometimes use surveys.

- When doing a survey, it's important that the people completing a questionnaire or answering interview questions are similar to the group of people the psychologist is interested in. That is representative.

- To answer questions about whether one thing causes another, psychologists use the scientific method. They have a hypothesis and gather data to test whether their hunches are true.

- A control group is a group of people in a study who don't get experimental treatment and are compared to those who do.

- Once a research study is done, more studies are needed to check the conclusions.

CHAPTER 9

Misunderstanding Science and the Problem of Sticky Beliefs

When scientists find interesting results, those results can sometimes be misunderstood, especially if they're exciting. This is just what happened in a study of whether music can make people smarter. Newspapers and television news reported that researchers had found listening to Mozart made folks smarter. This was big news! But it wasn't quite right. Scientists only looked at how people scored on simple tests like parts of an intelligence test. But people who heard about the results jumped to the conclusion that Mozart's music made people smarter. Then, the idea grew. People began to think classical music might improve all kinds of performance. Soon, classical music was being played during football practices. Parents played classical music for babies to help develop their brains.

Of course, the research wasn't about the effect of music on babies' brains or on football skills. In fact, when other researchers repeated the studies, they didn't even find that Mozart regularly led to improvements on the kinds of tests originally used.

But that didn't matter! The idea that such a simple thing could make babies smarter stuck. Baby-focused classical music sold like crazy! And the fact that classical music didn't really make babies smarter wasn't interesting news, so the press didn't report it. It seemed everyone just wanted to believe this easy shortcut to making babies smarter. And the company that made the classical music recordings for infants made hundreds of millions of dollars years after researchers had proof they didn't work.

The Misunderstanding of Science

You've learned a lot about how people make mistakes observing and interpreting things they see and hear. You've read about psychologists who have used scientific research to understand how and why such false conclusions can result. But wrong ideas can also happen when people don't understand how science works. People can jump to conclusions about causation when two events are correlated. They may misunderstand specific scientific findings or not understand that scientific findings need to be repeated.

When Reporters Get It Wrong

Confusing correlation with causation can easily result in incorrect beliefs. Even news stories often confuse the two. You've learned that for research results to show causation, a study needs to compare what happens when a procedure is applied to one group (the experimental group) but not another (the control group). These results are followed by more studies to confirm the original result.

Consider the following real news headlines collected by researchers Christopher Chabris and Daniel Simons:

- "Drop that BlackBerry! Multitasking May be Harmful"—The study being reported asked people to fill out a questionnaire about whether they often used their phones while using other devices. They found those who said they did perform worse on some thinking skills tests. While this correlation is interesting, it doesn't prove looking at more than one device caused poorer test scores.

- "Bullying Harms Kids' Mental Health"—While this sounds believable, to prove causation researchers would need two groups of kids: one group that is bullied as part of the experiment and one group that is not. But bullying kids for the sake of an experiment is not okay, especially if the researcher thought it might cause harm!

Confusing Correlation and Causation Can Be Dangerous to Health

Measles is an infectious and dangerous disease. In the past, most children in the United States caught it at some time. For many, it meant being miserable for a little while. Others developed serious complications (including blindness and swelling of the brain), or even death. That changed with the development of a vaccine to prevent measles. Doctors and parents celebrated this miracle of modern medicine. Almost all children in America were vaccinated. As a result, measles was almost wiped out.

Then, in the late 1990s people noticed that some young children seemed to develop Autism Spectrum Disorder (ASD) around the time they were given MMR (measles, mumps, rubella) vaccines. Some people jumped to the conclusion that the vaccine caused ASD. People then started to refuse the vaccine! Scientists hurried to test if the vaccine might be causing ASD. Despite studies done in different parts of the world using control groups, researchers could not prove that kids got ASD after being vaccinated. A possible alternative explanation was that symptoms of ASD are often observed in kids who are 1 to 2 years old, around the same age kids start getting vaccines. In other words, a correlation.

Why Can't Scientists Just Tell Us the Answer?

Climate scientists agree the world is getting hotter. They also agree this will lead to more intense weather, like hurricanes and floods. Sea levels will rise as glaciers melt due to Earth's warming. This threatens both humans and animals. But despite years of study, climate scientists can't say whether a specific tornado, flood, or hurricane happened because of global warming. How can scientists be so sure, and yet so unsure?

It's tempting to be critical, but keep in mind climate researchers often measure things that never happened before. You learned we all use patterns to understand the world around us, but it can be hard to see patterns when they first appear. When information about what happened in the past is missing, we can't really see changes in patterns. Scientists only realized recently that measures of changes in climate are important.

Past measurement of things like glacier size and the amount of water in the sea are incomplete, simply because scientists didn't know how important such data would be. Information on the many things that cause glaciers to melt rapidly was not known because it had never happened before (at least not since humans were there to measure it).

Science Is Like a Puzzle

The way science builds knowledge over time can also lead to misunderstanding. The process of science is far more than a bunch of facts discovered in a bunch of studies. New data may lead to changes in what was previously thought. Each study tries to answer small parts of bigger questions.

EXPLORE FURTHER
Search online to read about an argument between paleontologists Cope and Marsh. They disagreed about which end of a dinosaur was the front!

DID YOU KNOW?

For over 45 years the Carnegie Museum of Natural History displayed a dinosaur with the wrong head! For much of this time paleontologists did not realize the error. What happened? While digging for dino remains, paleontologists unearthed an almost intact dinosaur. It was only missing its head. A dino head nearby was thought to be too small. The find was exhibited headless but later a plaster cast of what the scientists believed—incorrectly— was the head of another example of this dinosaur was added. Later fossil discoveries made it clear a mistake had been made. In fact, that too small head is now known to be from this giant beast.

Scientists begin with **theories**, reasonable ideas about how the world works based on past knowledge and experience.

> **Theory:** a carefully considered explanation for something, based on observation and prior knowledge.

theory → hypothesis → testing → data → theory is supported

→ revise theory

Scientific research is a bit like assembling a dinosaur from a few fossils. Scientists develop a hypothesis (an idea to test) based on their best guesses about how things work. That hypothesis guides their research. They design experiments to test the hypothesis. Each research discovery adds to understanding big questions. Sometimes the pieces don't fit together in a way that supports their theory. That may mean the theory is incorrect, or at least that it needs tweaking. Bit by bit, study after study, scientists combine the pieces into a more complete whole.

The results of science research are never complete. There are some questions that science can't completely answer, and some they can't answer at all. As new evidence is discovered, what we know gets tweaked a bit. Face it, when you want answers, it can be hard to be patient with all the checking and rechecking of facts and evidence. But being patient leads to better understanding and means information is more trustworthy.

Why so many studies? There are a few reasons. One study may not be big enough to include all kinds of people. That may mean the findings won't apply to everyone. When psychologists begin to study a new question, they often use research participants who are easy to find. Since a lot of research is done at colleges, research participants in the first study may be students. College students may be too similar to each other in age and education, and different from most other people. This is a type of **sampling bias**.

> **Sampling bias:** the result of choosing research participants who do not represent a wide variety of people.

DID YOU KNOW?

Until recently, a lot of medical research used White men as research participants. But White male bodies aren't the only kind of bodies. And some illnesses are more common, or just different, in people of color. As a result of this sampling bias, knowledge about the medical needs of people other than White men was often not available.

Starting with a limited type of participants is not wrong, but the results may not fit everyone. Often, a promising line of research done in this way is followed by studies on more diverse groups to ensure the same results are found.

At other times, the question to be answered is complicated and the research needs to be broken into parts. Imagine you want to know how best to care for a house plant. You might want to explore how much light works best or what temperature is ideal. Maybe you're interested in how much water it needs and whether or not to fertilize it. You might also want to consider what "best" means. Is it care that leads to fast growth or that produces flowers? You couldn't test all of those at once. If you tried, you wouldn't know what was working or whether it was a combination of things.

Try This

Hot pink is a very eye-catching color. Imagine if researchers wanted to study if painting stop signs bright pink would result in more people obeying them.

If they do the reseach in a suburban neighborhood and find that hot pink signs do make more vehicles stop at intersections, can they assume the same will be true everywhere? Could it be different in places like busy cities with stop-and-go traffic? What about rural towns with hardly any traffic?

Another reason a single study doesn't result in solid facts is sometimes one study just gets it wrong. When a research study is repeated and the same result is found, scientists feel more confident the result is correct. But sometimes when an experiment is repeated by another researcher, they don't get the same results. This is called a **failure to replicate**. This is one way science guards against sticking with incorrect conclusions.

Failure to replicate: when a research study is repeated by others but fails to find the original results.

How Much of a Difference Makes A Difference?

You are a scientist who has been asked to find out whether kids prefer chocolate chip or peanut butter cookies. You carefully select 50 kids who do not have a peanut allergy, so your sample isn't biased by including kids who can't eat peanut butter cookies. You also make sure your sample includes kids of different ages. Your sample group includes boys, girls, and gender nonconforming kids. The same number of each type of cookie is put on a platter, and each kid gets to choose a cookie. Your results show 24 kids chose peanut butter and 26 chose chocolate chip. Does that mean chocolate chip cookies are the most popular? Is this enough of a difference? How likely is it a different group of kids would choose 26 peanut butter cookies and 24 chocolate chip?

At the end of an experiment, scientists decide if they can believe the results. They do a math calculation to measure **statistical significance**. This measurement makes sure what they found isn't just random chance or luck.

> **Statistical significance:** a measure (using math) that makes it seem sensible to accept results of an experiment as being more than just chance.

Sometimes Wrong Conclusions Happen

Have you heard about different learning styles? It is said some people learn best by seeing information, others by hearing it, and still others by touching and handling stuff. Maybe you have had a teacher or parent help you figure out your personal learning style.

But the idea that students learn best when taught in their own learning style is based on a misunderstanding of science. Specifically, of neuroscientific studies. It's true that different brain regions are more active when sound, sight, or touch is being processed. But research has not found matching kids to specific teaching and learning styles is helpful for most students.

You might prefer to listen to an audio book rather than reading the words on a page. That doesn't mean you are an audio learner and not a visual learner. Most kids learn through all their senses. In fact, using more than one learning approach works best for almost all students. But despite this clear evidence against learning styles, almost all teachers across the world believe this myth. It's a myth that is also taught in many high schools and colleges. How has such misinformation become so accepted? Why hasn't accurate information, based on research findings in education, changed the beliefs of millions of teachers?

It's Hard To Change Wrong Beliefs

It turns out the first ideas you have about how something works can be "sticky," even if they are false. People often hold onto false beliefs, despite mounds of evidence and reasonable arguments they are not true. The same things that lead someone to believe false information in the first place also interfere with changing their mind when they get new information. Beliefs that are tied to strong emotions are especially hard to change using facts and logic. Confirmation bias blocks acceptance of new information. And if the information came from a highly trusted source, forget about it! It is nearly impossible to shake that wrong belief.

Because what you learn first can be very sticky,

CHECK OUT THE RESEARCH

the order that you learn something can change what you think. A famous research study by Solomon Asch tested this. Two groups of research participants read one of the following lists of words about a fictional person:

Person A: intelligent—industrious—impulsive—critical—stubborn—envious

Person B: envious—stubborn—critical—impulsive—industrious—intelligent

Did you notice the words are exactly the same? Even so, participants had a better opinion of person A than person B. Person A has more positive sounding words first. Person B has more negative first words. It turns out first impressions matter—a lot.

It may make sense that someone would change their mind when given new facts showing what they thought they knew is actually wrong. But research suggests it's not that simple. Once a person believes something, it's hard to change their mind, even with facts.

— CHECK OUT THE RESEARCH —

When someone hears a message, it tends to stick, even if it's corrected later. Researchers Hollyn Johnson and Colleen Seifert tested this **continued-influence effect**. People in their study were told that a warehouse fire was caused when someone left gas cylinders and oil paints in a closet.

Some of the participants were later told they'd been given wrong information. They were told that in fact, the closet had been empty. But many still reported that false detail when they described the event. And they made this mistake even if they remembered being told it wasn't true.

Continued-influence effect: a tendency for false information to continue to be believed even when it has been retracted (taken back) or corrected.

The continued-influence effect does not just happen during scientific studies. In the real world, people sometimes hold to a belief even if they are told the information is false.

In 1957 advertising researcher James Vicary reported he had made a new discovery. He claimed flashing the words, "Drink Coca-Cola" and "Eat Popcorn" quickly during a movie would increase sales at the snack counter.

The images flashed too fast to be recognized, but Mr. Vicary said his study found they had a subliminal impact on viewers. Broadcasters and governments banned advertisers from using subliminal messages. When other researchers failed to replicate the results, Vicary admitted he had made it all up. He had not really done the studies at all. But people believed him anyway! Over the next 60 years many studies explored whether subliminal effects were real and didn't find them. But Vicary's surprising report that people could be so easily influenced is still believed today!

It can be difficult to correct misinformation. In fact, it may be harder than you'd think. Disagreeing with something a person has accepted as true may actually make that belief stronger. When you disagree with someone, it reminds them of what they believe. Instead of changing their minds, they may come up with reasons why you are wrong. This backfiring of corrective messages is called the **boomerang effect**.

> **Boomerang effect:** the strengthening of old beliefs when challenged by new, more accurate information. This may cue the listener to think about arguments against the new data.

Ever-Changing Scientific Knowledge

Research is always adding new information to the puzzle of knowledge. Because of this, scientific conclusions can change. This is especially true when scientists are trying to answer questions that haven't been explored in the past. Or when the research topic is something that is evolving. Climate change and health are two areas where scientists can often sound as if they are contradicting themselves. But really, different messages are due to new research findings. That's just what happened with Pluto.

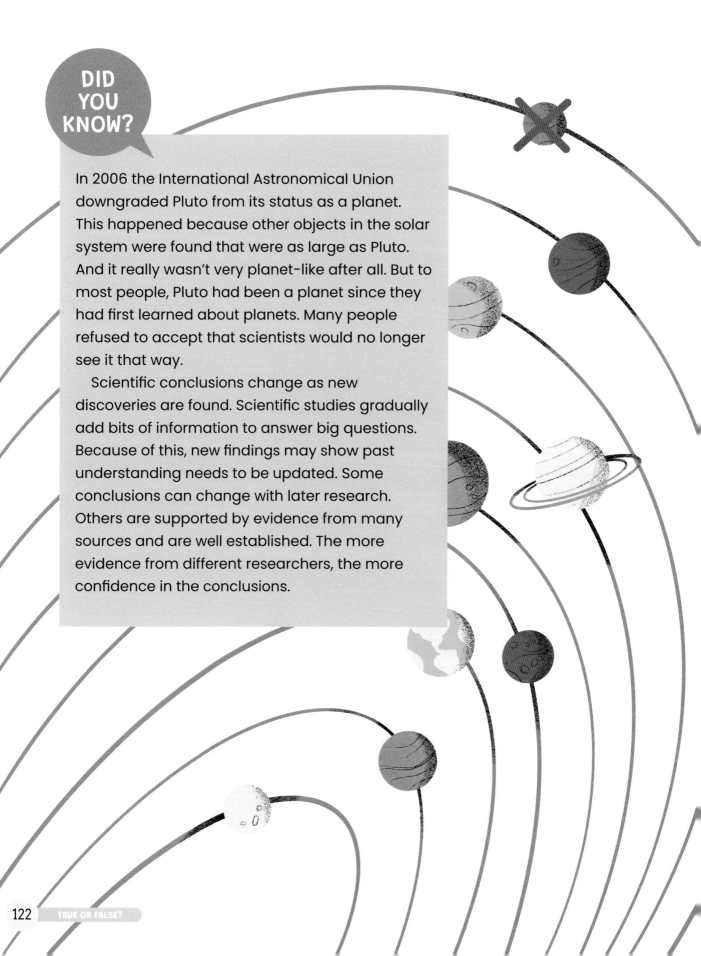

In 2006 the International Astronomical Union downgraded Pluto from its status as a planet. This happened because other objects in the solar system were found that were as large as Pluto. And it really wasn't very planet-like after all. But to most people, Pluto had been a planet since they had first learned about planets. Many people refused to accept that scientists would no longer see it that way.

Scientific conclusions change as new discoveries are found. Scientific studies gradually add bits of information to answer big questions. Because of this, new findings may show past understanding needs to be updated. Some conclusions can change with later research. Others are supported by evidence from many sources and are well established. The more evidence from different researchers, the more confidence in the conclusions.

Real World Impact

When someone is interviewed on the news, reporters may talk about whether what they said is true. Some news outlets have regular "fact checking" segments to look into whether information is backed by evidence. But as you learned in this chapter, providing corrections to wrong information may not be enough. You've seen how false ideas about vaccines resulted in some children not getting vaccines for measles. During the COVID-19 pandemic, false rumors about vaccines made some people refuse to get them. Even untrue ideas that led to life-threatening results proved "sticky."

Incorrect beliefs can influence not only health decisions, but also things like the best way for teachers to teach. They can influence how to help people in poverty and how to address climate change. Incorrect beliefs can even influence understanding about what happened in history. If such errors are not easily corrected by more accurate facts, we are all at risk of making mistakes in the choices we make.

Scientific knowledge changes over time, and this can cause confusion. Sometimes misunderstanding science can lead to the spread of misunderstanding. Such errors may be accidental. But, as you will see in the next chapters, sometimes misinterpretation of science is used to purposely mislead people. Understanding that one scientific finding is not proof of a fact, but only a bit of evidence along the way, is important. It may help you avoid the trap of believing something that isn't true!

Now You Know

- Jumping to conclusions based on a single research finding can lead to incorrect conclusions.

- Scientific research provides evidence that may or may not support an underlying theory. Each study is just one piece in a larger puzzle. Scientists use statistics (math) to understand whether their findings are meaningful or may be due to chance.

- Inaccurate conclusions about scientific results are sometimes picked up by the media and can become widely believed.

- Misunderstandings of scientific findings can be very difficult to correct. Sometimes efforts to do so can even strengthen the false belief.

CHAPTER 10

Rumors, Conspiracy, and Other Misinformation

It's raining very hard, and the wind is blowing. On the way to school, you pass a big traffic accident. There are two ambulances, a fire truck, and three police cars on the scene. A mangled car sits on the side of the road and a truck with a crushed front is facing in the wrong direction. When you arrive at school, will you tell your friends about the accident and all its details or that you wish you'd worn a raincoat because you got soaking wet?

Misinformation: incorrect or misleading information that can result in others being misinformed. Misinformation may be spread without the intention to mislead other people.

If you're like most people, you'll talk about the accident. And it's likely your story will include the most dramatic details, like flashing lights, an injured person on a stretcher, and crunched vehicles. Less exciting details like there were four people who appeared unhurt and were talking calmly to a police officer might be trimmed from the story. You might also share your thoughts on how the accident happened, even though you didn't see it. Or maybe you'll include details you heard from someone else at the scene.

Rumor: a story or statement passed from person to person without evidence about whether it is true or invented.

Sometimes innocent errors that result from trying to tell a good story can result in **misinformation**. Other times, misinformation comes in the form of **rumors**, something someone heard secondhand. At other times, facts (including scientific research) that have been misunderstood are the source of misinformation.

125

You Won't Believe What Happened! Or Will You?

She must have fainted!

Rumors can start when something happens that raises emotions. It's not likely a rumor would start about a girl in your class who failed to tie her shoelace for gym class. But if she tripped over her laces and fell down a flight of stairs and was hurt, and an ambulance came, rumors about what happened might start to spread. And, if they did, the stories might not be completely accurate.

An exciting story that includes details added (or left out) might then be passed on to family members, friends, friends of friends, and even strangers. This type of misinformation is unintended but can spread untruths. Rumors of very emotional happenings spread quickly, whether they are true or not.

CHECK OUT THE RESEARCH

What makes us want to share a story? We know emotions include physical responses in the body. When strong emotions kick in, your body may react with a racing heart, sweating, dilating eyes, shaking, and so on. Psychologist Jonah Berger wondered if it might be this physical revving up that prompts people to share information.

He used two experimental groups. One group saw an emotion-charged video. The other group revved up their bodies by jogging. Control groups for both groups engaged in calm activities.

Guess what? Both the joggers and the folks who watched the high-drama video shared more information than the control (calm activities) groups. It seemed the bodily feelings led people to connect and share with others.

From Misunderstandings to Conspiracy Theories

Have you ever heard of a **conspiracy theory**? A conspiracy theory is an idea that powerful people are keeping a secret or causing something to happen secretly. Conspiracy theories sometimes grow out of a coincidence (correlation). Usually, it's after something bad or upsetting happens. People may search through ideas they already believe and try to find a pattern that helps it all make sense. That might mean worries and fears mix with rumors and become woven into a story about other people, often people in power, who are working against them. While sometimes conspiracy theories can seem strange to others, the people who believe them really think they are true. Once a conspiracy theory is believed, anything that fits that story seems convincing. Evidence that it is wrong is ignored. You know, confirmation bias kicks in!

> **Conspiracy theory:** a theory suggesting a powerful group is keeping something hidden from the public or has caused an event to occur.

DID YOU KNOW?

The following are all conspiracy theories people truly believe, despite the facts:

- There was never a moon landing. It was all faked by the government.
- An alien spaceship crashed in New Mexico in 1947, but the information was hidden by the government.
- President Obama was born in Kenya and, therefore, wasn't legally allowed to be president.

You may have heard of the Salem witch trials during colonial times. A couple of hundred people were accused of being witches. Thirty people were convicted and 19 were even put to death for this "crime."

Do some research about what happened. Think about what you've learned about how misinformation happens. How might confusion between correlation and causation, seeing patterns that don't exist, confirmation bias, social pressure, and interesting story telling convince people that someone was a witch? Do you think strong emotions like fear might have interfered with clear thinking?

Scary Stories Grab Attention?

Why would anyone choose to grasp onto a frightening theory, one that suggests there are hidden forces controlling the world? Wouldn't simpler, less frightening explanations be easier to accept? Research studies have found a number of psychological factors that contribute to belief in conspiracies. People may be convinced of a **conspiracy** because it provides an explanation for something that doesn't seem to make sense. If they are feeling afraid, they may be on the lookout for threats (you know, automatic vigilance) in order to protect themselves. Or, a conspiracy theory may help them feel good about themselves and a group they belong to.

When information is confusing, conflicting, or incomplete, a conspiracy theory gives people an explanation that seems to explain why something happened (the cause). This can make the world seem less unpredictable. Suddenly a pattern becomes clear (remember, we all like patterns).

Conspiracy: a secret plot formed by two or more people.

Why would someone believe in a conspiracy?

To make sense of a scary event

To identify danger

To fit into a group to fight "wrong-doers"

Suggesting some hidden group is responsible may allow people to reject messages which threaten prior beliefs, since new information is seen as coming from an untrustworthy source. Plus, having someone to blame means there's an enemy, someone (or some group) to defend against. Conspiracy theories also help people feel they belong to a group. A group (other believers in the conspiracy) who are right, while outsiders are to blame for bad things that happen.

Misinformation Can Be Sticky

Some rumors are repeated so much that lots of people believe they're true! Have you ever heard (or believed) these **urban myths**?

Urban myth: a strange or shocking falsehood that isn't true but is widely known and shared.

- If you find a baby bird that's fallen from its nest you shouldn't touch it because its parents will abandon it if they smell humans. (Birds won't abandon their chicks just because they notice human scents on them.)

- Dogs only see in black and white. (Dogs don't see all the colors we do, but they do see colors.)

- Bananas grow on trees. (While banana plants can grow as tall as a tree, banana plants are more like orchids or lilies. Their stems are formed of tightly packed leaves and the bananas are the plant's berries.)

- The Great Wall of China can be seen from space. (Although it's huge, the Great Wall cannot be seen from space.)

- The way to treat a sting from a jelly fish is to pee on it. (NO! It won't help and could result in more toxins from the jellyfish being released. Besides, it's gross!)

Why do humans so easily accept what they hear? Sometimes it's because they hear it when they're distracted by other things. If you're upset, focused on an activity, exercising, or being rushed you may not be paying close enough attention to think things through. When you can't think things through, it's just easier to accept what you hear.

Kids prefer walking to bike riding.

Try This

Texting is a fast and easy way to communicate information. How might this very advantage of speedy sharing contribute to spreading untrue rumors? Might quick responses to texts also result in sharing information a person may regret later? Have you ever sent a text and wished you could take it back?

You Don't Know What You Don't Know

When confronted with different "facts," some true and some misleading, what do people believe? To some degree it depends on how much they think they know already. We all have things we know and things we know we don't. When we know that we know very little about something, we're more likely to be open to information about it. But how good are people at knowing what they know and don't know?

This is where things get weird! It turns out human beings can be really bad at knowing how much they do and don't know. People who know a little about a topic often feel super confident about their knowledge, while those who know a lot about the subject often aren't!

CHECK OUT THE RESEARCH

David Dunning and Justin Kruger tested people on their skills in three areas: logic, grammar, and humor. Those who were worst at these skills overestimated their abilities (a lot!) compared to people who were better at them.

It could be that less informed people simply have no idea there's a lot more to learn. People who have a lot of knowledge, however, may have a better sense that their knowledge is just part of a bigger picture. After all, to know what you don't know requires you to at least know that there's more to know! There's even a name for this. It's called the **Dunning-Kruger effect**, after the researchers who discovered it.

Dunning-Kruger effect: when people with limited knowledge or skills in an area tend to overestimate their knowledge and underestimate what they don't know.

Confused? Well, consider the game of chess. Someone who is just learning to play chess may find it challenging to remember what moves each piece can make. Once they have mastered that and played a few games, they may start to understand some pieces are more powerful than others. They may begin to feel more confident about how to play the game.

But as people progress to higher levels of play, they become aware that true masters do far more than practice playing chess. Chess masters read books about famous games and learn strategies that include not just the next move but several moves ahead. To someone trying to improve their game it may seem the more one knows about chess, the more there is to learn.

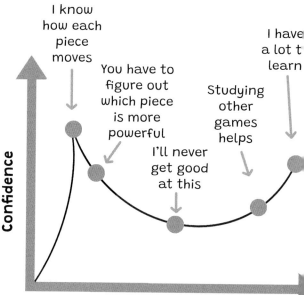

It's easy to be fooled by someone who speaks with great authority about a subject. Unless there is reason to believe they have expertise on the topic, it may be a good idea to check the facts they present.

Real World Impact

You learned how some people came to the incorrect conclusion that childhood vaccines for measles caused Autism Spectrum Disorder (ASD). During the COVID-19 pandemic members of this group started a campaign against the vaccine developed to combat that virus. Some of what they said focused on conspiracy theories. They said individuals or groups were using the vaccine to permanently change a person's genes or even implant microchips so those who were vaccinated could be followed by the government. But they also presented more believable sounding "proof" of the dangers of the vaccines, including examples of individuals who had died shortly after receiving the vaccine. Baseball legend Hank Aaron was one such person.

But the evidence used was not based on scientific studies. As with the MMRI vaccines and ASD, evidence against vaccines showed correlation, not causation. Dr. Paul Offit, who directs the Vaccine Education Center at the Children's Hospital of Philadelphia noted, "Hank Aaron gets the vaccine. Two weeks later he dies of a stroke. Why? Because he was in his late 80s, and people in their late 80s can die of strokes. The vaccine doesn't make you immortal."

Now You Know

- Misinformation can result from misunderstanding of information. False conclusions can then be passed along to others.

- Rumors can result when emotionally charged information is distorted and spread.

- Jumping to conclusions about causation can result in many types of incorrect conclusions. When combined with other thinking errors it can result in beliefs in conspiracies. Sometimes misinformation is repeated so frequently it becomes an urban myth.

- A person's confidence in their own skill or knowledge is not a good measure of their actual ability. In fact, those who know just a small amount about a subject may be quite sure of their expertise, in part because they don't know how much more there is to learn.

CHAPTER 11 ?

Lies, Falsehoods, and Fake Experts (or Disinformation)

A lot of misinformation happens by accident. Often, people believe what they pass along and have just misunderstood. But sometimes, people lie or twist the truth on purpose. This is called **disinformation**. And disinformation can be super sticky, which can make it hard to correct.

For example, what if you heard mouthwash could cure (or prevent) the common cold? For over 50 years advertisements for Listerine mouthwash claimed it could. But it wasn't true. A court told the company to correct these lies. And it did. For over a year, Listerine ads said it couldn't cure colds or reduce the chance of getting them. But people continued to believe it could. Remember what you learned about the *continued-influence effect*. Are you surprised people didn't correct their beliefs? Probably not. A survey found more than half of Listerine customers said they still bought it to avoid colds. And the makers of Listerine continued to make money from their false claims, despite being caught and making the correction.

What happened with Listerine is an example of a company using lies or twisted facts to spread disinformation for their own gain. Sometimes the goal of disinformation is to make money or gain power. Other times it is to convince people to agree with opinions.

Disinformation: purposeful misinformation. Falsehoods that are deliberately spread to deceive others. Often people spreading disinformation can profit financially, professionally, or politically.

Have you ever seen *The Wizard of Oz*? If so, you've seen disinformation in action. During the first part of the movie a man travels around in a wagon selling cures for all types of illnesses and aches. Later, he becomes the Wizard. He has become an important man in the land of Oz, with great powers. The only thing is, his powers are completely fake. He used disinformation to gain power and fame.

Try This

E-cigarettes are another example. At first, they were developed for people trying to break a cigarette addiction. But pretty soon, e-cigarettes with fruity flavors were marketed by social influencers who were popular with kids. Vaping by young people increased.

How might flavoring e-cigarettes with fruity flavors make them seem different from cigarettes? Can you imagine how that might confuse young people about whether they are safe or not? Do you think the attractive way they were represented might create a positive impression of vaping? How might that interfere with careful thinking about using tobacco?

Fake Experts

In Chapter 2, you learned that people tend to believe experts. But what makes an expert? How do you know when an expert is actually an expert?

During a news program in Australia, two people debated whether climate change was real or not. Both people claimed to be weather experts. Turns out, neither of them was. One person had worked with governments on climate change, but he wasn't a scientist. And the other said he had become an expert from observing storms while fishing. It seemed weather was not the only thing he claimed to be an expert about. He also claimed to be an expert on telling the future by looking at cats' paws. In fact, he had written a book on fortune-telling through reading a cat's palm!

Although some fake experts are obvious, some can be harder to spot. And when the result is disinformation about health, it can be dangerous. Past messages about tobacco are a perfect example.

Today the dangers of smoking are widely known and accepted. That wasn't always the case. In fact, at one time people believed smoking was healthy! When research showed smoking was bad for the lungs and heart, tobacco companies ignored it. They even hid their own research about the dangers. During the 1980s, cigarette companies used "scientific experts" to reassure people about smoking's safety. But these people were not experts at all. In fact, they were actors! The companies didn't actually lie about who they were. But having them dress like scientists in white lab coats convinced listeners they were experts.

Using **fake experts** to challenge scientific findings happens more often than you might think. The claims they make can sound convincing. Often, there's no way to know if the person has done any studies on the topic. Or how much money they could make from the product they are promoting. You might be less convinced to buy a brain-boosting pill if you learned the person selling it was an actor who didn't know what was in it. And you'd probably be even more suspicious if you learned the more brain-boosters the actor sold, the more money they'd make.

Fake experts: unqualified sources of information.

Even Experts Don't Know Everything

Sometimes disinformation comes from an expert in a subject that has nothing to do with what they are promoting. Take a well-known United States heart surgeon that was also a TV personality. He gave advice to millions of viewers. Much of his advice had nothing to do with heart surgery, something he did actually know about. For example, he spread false claims that children's apple juice contained dangerous levels of a poison called arsenic. He falsely claimed that genetically modified foods cause cancer. And he made a false claim that a mixture of vinegar, honey, and juice was a miracle weight loss potion. This disinformation was so misleading that a group of other doctors complained. Eventually, the heart surgeon was brought before the United States Congress. He was scolded for presenting disinformation to his viewers.

EXPLORE FURTHER
Search online for "outrageous vintage cigarette ads." It's surprising to see who tobacco companies put in ads to make smoking seem safe and fun!

Take this tiny pill to get straight As without even studying! Just send me $99!

Try This

Both sides of the abortion issue have been labeled. You probably know one side is called "pro-life." And the other is "pro-choice." The names depend on the point of view of the speaker. What different emotions do you think listeners might have when they hear those words? Would anyone agree with an "anti-life" or "anti-choice" position?

Words Matter

The specific words someone uses can change the impact of their message. Some words have strong emotional associations. These associations can affect people's reactions. Politicians are aware of this. Often, they choose words that trigger strong reactions to gain support for their positions.

For example, different people used different names for the Civil War. In the past, Union officials called the conflict "the war to preserve the Union." Those words probably made people feel patriotic. Confederates called it "the war to defend states' rights." Those words may have made people feel their rights were being threatened.

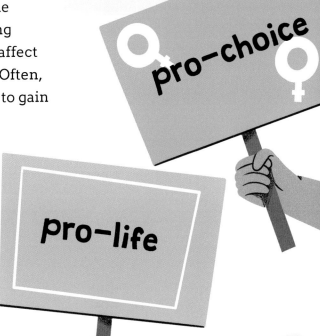

Sometimes words that have been used in one way for a long time can be twisted. Often, this happens by people who disagree with the original use. This can make communication confusing. One example is "fake news." At first, this phrase meant news reports that contained disinformation. Later, it was used to undermine news reports that people disagreed with. This happened even when the reports were based on facts.

I'm Just Asking

It's not always necessary to **lie** to spread disinformation. In fact, disinformation can be spread just by asking a question. When a question hints at something, but doesn't state it, beware! Does that question use a bit of truth to suggest something that isn't true? It might be disinformation. Especially if the person asking doesn't have facts to support what they're implying. Or if they can't even answer their own question!

Lie: an untrue statement designed to mislead someone.

Disinformation spread through questions can be used to challenge scientific evidence when there is no proof that the data are wrong. One example is climate change. Scientists had evidence that overall, Earth's atmosphere was warming. And that global warming was expected to lead to changes in weather. But some people didn't believe the facts. They sometimes asked why was there a record cold day today if Earth was warming? Spreading doubt isn't hard to do. Especially because science is almost never conclusive.

I'm not a scientist, but why would we have all this snow if global warming is real?

WHAT?!

As you learned! People who challenged climate change did not do the hard work of science. They didn't give evidence to create doubt. They just asked questions.

When the Argument Doesn't Add up

Think about this statement: "More boys play team sports than girls. Therefore, boys are born more athletic." This is an example of a **logical fallacy**. It's a fancy way of saying the conclusion doesn't follow from the argument. A logical fallacy happens when someone presents an idea and says it leads to a conclusion, when it really doesn't. It's illogical. Can you think of any reasons why boys might play more team sports than girls? There are many. Like what others might expect. Or if teams are available for both boys and girls.

Logical fallacy: an argument drawing on incomplete evidence to reach a conclusion that sounds sensible but isn't logical.

Consider the following logical fallacies:

- If we start banning cars that use a lot of gas, soon we'll have to walk everywhere.
- Julie had an allergic reaction to pineapples, so we should all stop eating pineapples.
- More women are stay-at-home parents than men, so women aren't meant to work.

What are these illogical conclusions missing? What other examples can you think of?

You already know a bunch of ways people reach false conclusions. Sometimes these are purposely wrapped in logical fallacies to mislead people. This kind of disinformation may be used by people who can make money or gain power by influencing others. Claiming that a correlation proves causation is one type of logical fallacy. Suggesting everyone thinks a certain way, even when it isn't true, is another. Attacking someone for something unrelated to the argument is also an illogical way to "win."

Just ignore it! After all, they are just a little kid.

Cherry Picking

Logical fallacies are one way someone can twist information. But there are others. Sometimes disinformation depends on the listener misunderstanding science. That misunderstanding can convince them of an untrue conclusion.

Let's say your friend is a fan of the Let's Go soccer team. They insist they are the best team ever! You root for the Woo-hoos and think they are awesome. Your friend brags that Let's Go beat Woo-hoo 3-1 last week. But the Woo-hoos won 5 of the last 6 matchups. Why might your friend only want to talk about that last game? They are **cherry picking** to make their point. Only using a small amount of evidence in their argument while ignoring the fact that it's not true overall is cherry picking. Your friend used it to present a false view of which team is stronger.

HOME	GUEST
3	**1**

Cherry picking: selecting data that seems to support one position and ignoring data that contradicts it.

People who want to distort facts sometimes cherry pick scientific studies. You learned scientific conclusions change over time as more research is done. One research result never settles a question. Findings must be repeated by different scientists, under different circumstances, to answer a scientific question. And it's rare for results to be exactly the same across studies. If many studies show one result, but a few don't agree, scientists are still pretty confident in their conclusions. But sometimes those isolated results are used to spread disinformation and argue against conclusions proven over and over.

melting glaciers

average yearly temperature

threatened species

it's snowing

declining insects

extreme weather

Demanding That Science Has Answers

Scientists are sometimes criticized for not having definite answers. But you know that's just how science works! It's normal for research conclusions to come with a bit of doubt. Scientists (and you) understand knowledge is gained bit by bit. And new findings can show old conclusions are incomplete or wrong.

Disinformation can twist this to make it look like science isn't helpful at all. Some people exaggerate scientists' caution when evidence is presented that doesn't support their argument.

For example, climate scientists talk about how storms are more intense and generally happen more often. This has allowed some climate change deniers to create doubt in people's minds.

Scientists are collecting data that shows that storms and fires are more frequent and intense as the planet is getting hotter.

Yeah, climate change deniers like to twist information and use it to support their own conclusions.

When Numbers Lie

Numbers can be pretty convincing things. After all, data presented as percentages, rates, or in charts or graphs is evidence. But the way numbers are presented can sometimes be misleading.

Try This

Health professionals sometimes talk about the health benefits of eating less fat. Consider a billboard on a farm advertising the fresh milk they are selling is 97% fat free. This makes this farm's milk sound like a good choice for someone trying to eat less fat. Are you convinced?

In fact, all whole milk is 97% fat free. The ad is just saying it in a way we aren't used to. But it isn't just a change of words. The sign maker is counting on us probably making a quick choice when choosing milk. They are counting on the fact that numbers presented as data or evidence can be used to legitimize claims. (By the way, low-fat milk is 98% or 99% fat-free, while skim milk is 100% fat-free. Now you know!)

Our milk is 97% fat-free

It's easy to be confused by percentages. Carl Bergstrom and Jevin West are biologists interested in how data are used to misinform the public. They use the example of an advertisement selling a soda that is 99.9% caffeine free. Sounds pretty healthy. Certainly better than a drink from a coffee shop, right? Turns out caffeine only makes up about .1% of the ingredients in all coffee and soda. They have a lot more in them than caffeine! A regular coffee from your local coffee shop is also 99.9% caffeine free. The rest is other stuff (mostly water)! That "low caffeine" drink isn't really low in caffeine at all. The advertisement used a true percentage to fool the public into thinking something that wasn't true.

Sometimes advertisers present impressive sounding numbers to convince people to buy their products. While the numbers they use may be true, they can be misleading. In 2007 Colgate-Palmolive ran an advertisement saying 80% of dentists recommended their toothpaste. Sounds like it was preferred by most dentists, doesn't it? What the advertisement didn't say was dentists in the survey could recommend many kinds of toothpaste. They didn't have to choose a favorite. So, Colgate may not have been any more preferred (or even less preferred) than other brands.

Okay, this part is going to get a bit technical—turn on your learning caps! The disinformation used in these examples comes from the lack of statistical **base rates**. While it sounds like these products are great, we don't know anything about what "normal" expectations are for similar products. The information presented doesn't tell us much about whether these products are better than, equivalent to, or even worse than other choices.

Base rates: how often something usually happens. This rate can be compared to the rate under experimental conditions.

Graphs can distort base rates to make small differences seem large. Let's say we want to know if a new band called The Clangors is more popular than another band, Smash Its. A survey asks 200 kids which band they prefer. The Clangor's agent says this graph proves their band is more popular. Can you spot the problems with his claim?

A quick look could make it seem like The Clangors have twice as many fans. But there's something weird about this graph. The number of Likes only goes to 115. This exaggerates the apparent differences between the Clangors and the Smash Its. A more accurate graph would look like this:

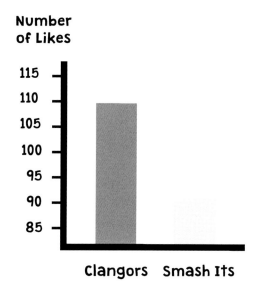

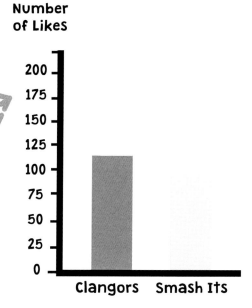

Both graphs show the same information, but viewers may get very different ideas from them. By leaving out some data, a tiny difference is made to look big.

Hiding Information Is a Kind of Disinformation

You learned people can lie or distort facts to mislead others. Sometimes hiding information is used as a type of disinformation, too. Remember how tobacco companies hid evidence that smoking was dangerous to health? In the 1980s, oil companies also hid information about serious problems. Exxon and Shell Oil scientists warned company executives about the dangers to the climate of burning fossil fuels. But the companies hid the information from the public and the government.

When Pictures Lie

Have you ever made changes to a digital photograph? Maybe you took a selfie and made your eyes look super big! Or you might have made your image turn into an animal. It can be fun to play around with changing digital pictures. But when photos are changed in ways that look believable, they can be used to spread disinformation. And they can be very convincing!

CHECK OUT THE RESEARCH

Sam Wineburg and colleagues showed high school students photographs of flowers that had been weirdly distorted. The caption read, "Fukushima Nuclear Flowers: Not much more to say, this is what happens when flowers get nuclear birth defects."

Most of the students (80%) were convinced the digital pictures were proof that a nuclear accident caused the strange flower growth. They didn't question where the photo was taken or under what circumstances.

Artificial Intelligence can create videos of people saying all kinds of things. And sometimes these "people" aren't real. They are avatars created by computers. Recently, some of these avatars have been used to try to spread misinformation and disinformation.

Artificial Intelligence (AI): human-like thinking processes done by computers.

Try This

It can often be hard to spot an altered photograph. But sometimes the photo itself, or the context, can offer clues. Less reputable publications sometimes change pictures when reporting a sensational story. Watch for these clues:

- Does it say where the image came from? Is that source trustworthy?

- Are there signs it was taken in a place or time different than claimed?

- Is there anything weird or inconsistent about how shadows and light fall? Do people's positions seem strange? This can be a sign a photo is a combination of more than one image.

Altered photographs and pictures taken in a different context can present false information about real events. In 2017 a group of protestors gathered to oppose an oil pipeline threatening a Native American community. The group set up camp near the Standing Rock Sioux reservation. In February of that year, protestors were ordered by the federal government to leave the camp, which was at risk of flooding. Many people across the United States were sympathetic to the demonstrators. People strongly felt the Sioux's resources should be protected. Emotions ran high. Disinformation began to spread. A rumor started that the police had raided the camp and set the protestors' tents on fire to drive the activists away. Soon a photograph of flaming tents circulated. The photo was real but was not from Standing Rock. In fact, the activists had left on their own. The photo was really a scene from a movie.

Of course, it can be very hard to tell whether a photograph has been changed. The best bet is to research whether it fits with other evidence.

Now You Know

- Misinformation can result from accidental errors.

- Disinformation is sometimes used by people who might make money or get power from pushing false information.

- Before accepting expert information it's important to be sure the source has expertise in the topic.

- Emotionally charged words are sometimes used to distort ideas.

- Accurate information is sometimes distorted by

  - Illogical conclusions
  - Cherry picking facts
  - Twisting the meaning of scientific findings
  - Presenting misleading numbers to support an argument

- Digitally manipulated photographs are a form of disinformation and can be hard to recognize.

CHAPTER 12

Social Media Influence: Forces for Good and...Not So Good

People like to talk about other people. That's probably been true since humans began to speak! You've already learned that as rumors spread, details drop out and others are added. The truth can get lost in the process. And the internet and social media can make this happen at supersonic speed! Sometimes stories change in ways that don't matter that much. But when misinformation and disinformation are added, rumors can hurt. Sometimes they can be dangerous, or even deadly.

Many things that go viral are fun or just silly. But sometimes viral rumors lead to conspiracy theories. Take an example from 2016. Former first lady Hillary Clinton was running for president. A casual comment made by people who did not think she should be president started a false rumor online. And it was mean. Her political enemies spread the story and made-up details. At the same time other countries were trying to disrupt the American election. Those countries spread even more extreme lies about Mrs. Clinton. Eventually, all this disinformation led to a bizarre conspiracy theory about her. The untrue rumor said Mrs. Clinton was kidnapping children and holding them in the basement of a pizza shop in Washington, D.C. The false story also said she planned to sell the children into slavery.

Protesters picketed the pizza shop. The owner got death threats. Then a man came with a gun. He planned to save the kidnapped children from the basement. He entered the kitchen and shot at one of the workers. Luckily, he missed. But there were no children in the basement. There never had been. In fact, the restaurant didn't even have a basement! The story had no truth to it, but it spread over social media and put real lives in danger.

This example is extreme, but many false stories spread on the internet and other forms of social media.

— Internet and Social Media

The internet is amazing. We can find all kinds of information quickly and easily. This also makes misinformation and disinformation super easy to find. It's not that false information doesn't exist out in the real world. But the internet can share information far and wide, very very fast. And no one is checking if the info is true.

Anyone can post whatever they want on the internet or on social media. Those who want to spread disinformation on purpose can do it easily.

Try This

How does the spread of online rumors relate to online bullying? Do you think people may say things online they wouldn't say face-to-face? How might a story become exaggerated as it passes from person to person? (Remember that game of telephone from Chapter 7?) Might hearing the same rumor from a bunch of people make it seem more believable?

Unlike books, newspapers, or trusted news shows, the internet does not have a **gatekeeping** mechanism. It doesn't have a way to fact-check information for accuracy before it is made available to the public. This means a lot of what you read or see online or on social media might not be reliable. Or exactly true. And some people can take advantage of that to spread disinformation.

Gatekeeping: the process of selecting and filtering information before it is presented to the public.

During the COVID-19 pandemic, a small number of people spread a whole lot of disinformation. Some of it dangerous. The nonprofit, Center for Countering Digital Hate, identified a dozen "super spreaders" of false information. There was even a doctor who sold natural "cures" for the virus. He hired people to go on social media and push the idea that vaccines didn't work, and people should use his (ineffective) treatments instead. He made a lot of money! He also discouraged people from getting effective protection from the disease.

DID YOU KNOW?

When Wikipedia first started it was considered unreliable. But as it's grown in popularity its crowd-sourced information, source lists, and cross references offer much more fact-checking.

Try This

You've heard lots of references to information "going viral" online. Imagine you have a taco truck and need customers. Write an online message to get people to check out your tacos. Draw a diagram to show how your message is quickly shared and could go viral.

How many people have learned about the taco truck after you've done this five times?

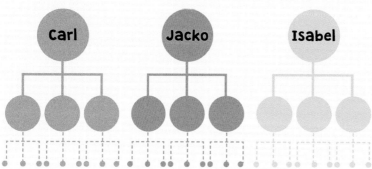

Social media platforms encourage people to like or share what they see. Stories, videos, or memes may be shared again and again. Because of how easy it is to share, posts that are far from true can go viral in a snap. Think about familiarity bias from Chapter 3. Information you've heard before is easier to accept. If you see the same thing repeated again and again, it starts to seem familiar and easier to believe. If that information is shared by lots of people, suddenly it seems everyone believes it (a false consensus effect). As incorrect information spreads and is shared, suddenly it is accepted as true by a large number of people!

CHECK OUT THE RESEARCH

People sometimes believe conspiracy theories to feel in control in a frightening situation. But it can work both ways. Believing a conspiracy theory can also lead people to feel threatened. And it might make them feel overwhelmed and powerless.

Daniel Jolley and Karen Douglas told research subjects that climate change was a government hoax (a false conspiracy theory). They found that, after being exposed to this idea, participants were less likely to say they would try to reduce carbon use (like driving their car or flying on airplanes) than people who had not heard the conspiracy theory. In this and related studies, the researchers found that hearing conspiracy theories made people feel overwhelmed. The problem seemed too big and they felt anything they did wouldn't matter.

Not only that, but after hearing a conspiracy theory about one topic, people were less likely to trust any official information, even if it had nothing to do with the first conspiracy theory. Could it be that learning about conspiracy theories makes people think they can't trust people in charge? Or even that the truth doesn't matter?

How You Search Can Change What You See

When you look something up on the internet, sometimes you find two pieces of conflicting information. So, now what? Which source is most reliable and believable?

Your approach to a computer search can have a big impact on what turns up. How do you ask a question? What words do you put into the search engine? Which information and what sources do you believe?

Let's say someone simply wants to find factual information for a school research paper, they are choosing sources they feel are most likely to give them truthful information. This is called **accuracy motivation**. They may also consider how the information is being presented—Is it based on research studies or on personal anecdotes? Does it seem factual or is it someone's opinion? If they find surprising new information that comes from a well-researched and unbiased source, it may change what they understood before.

Accuracy motivation: when a person searching for new information is working to understand what is true.

I knew they were wrong about that!

But sometimes, what a person already thinks can influence how they search. They may look for things to prove a point. This **directional motivation** results in only being interested in information that fits what they already think. This is a type of confirmation bias. (Remember trying to prove cats are better than dogs in Chapter 6?) If new information doesn't fit what they think, out the window it goes! They will search until they find information that proves what they thought all along.

Consider how different people might react to a report by the National Academy of Sciences. This actual study used satellite images to study CO_2 levels in the atmosphere. Researchers found CO_2 levels in the atmosphere decreased when people travelled less during the COVID-19 pandemic. In other words, it seemed people flew and drove less, reducing the threat to the planet.

How might a person who wants accurate information react? How could this change their behavior? What about someone who wants to prove it was okay to start visiting family who lived far away? Or someone who wants to travel overseas? Would finding that this difference wasn't that important kick in? Might they dismiss the study? Would they change their travel plans?

When someone has a strong belief, they push hard to find information that supports what they think. It can interfere with understanding facts right in front of them. Even if they're super smart!

> **Directional motivation:** when a person seeking new information is only interested in what fits what they already believe.

CHECK OUT THE RESEARCH

Dan Kahan and colleagues studied how strong beliefs could interfere with rational thinking about new information. They took two groups of people who had strong but opposite beliefs about gun control. First, they tested everyone to see how good they were at understanding data presented in graphs. They asked both groups to look at complicated graphs of data pretending to show how well a new skin cream worked (something they didn't feel strongly about). They measured how well each participant understood that evidence.

Then the researchers relabeled some of the graphs. Now the same graphs seem to show how gun laws related to rates of crime (a topic people tend to have strong feelings about). This time, people said the data fit what they already thought about guns. They understood the evidence that way even when the graphs indicated they were wrong. And even more surprising, people who had done really well reading the graphs about skin cream were actually *more* likely to think the graphs on gun control supported their view when that wasn't true. It turns out being good at careful thinking may not be enough to overcome motivated reasoning when strong emotions are involved.

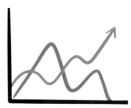

The Internet Thinks It Knows What You Want To Know

Okay, so you know you can't believe everything you see online. When you search for information online, some of what you see is true while some is not. How do you figure out which is which?

There are no easy answers, but it can help to know what happens when you search online. Some people assume when they put a topic or question into a search engine, the first things to pop up will be the most helpful and accurate. WRONG! What you see as first "hits" is influenced by what else you've looked at online. Search engines and websites gather all kinds of information about you. They also find information about your friends and what they like. In fact, search engines and social media sites are designed to show you some things and hide others. It's a bias that's built into the systems through their use of **algorithms**.

Algorithms are a set of programming instructions designed to choose which information is most likely to fit what you want. They are not based on thoughtful consideration. And they don't judge the accuracy of information. As we interact with search engines, they collect information about us. They do this through who we talk to and what we look for online, what we "like," and what we buy. This data goes into the algorithms used to make decisions about what we might prefer to see. So, if two people search the same topic but have a different history of online behavior, they may get different results. Think about that! Search engines have built-in confirmation bias! These algorithms contribute to people living in "information bubbles." That means they only get information that supports what they already think.

Algorithm: a process or set of rules that a computer program follows to solve a problem.

Don't blame me, I'm only finding info based on your search history!

Search engines, like Google or Firefox, keep their algorithms secret. They do this for two main reasons. First, it's a business secret so other companies can't copy them. Second, if people knew how it worked, others could interfere and make it less useful. But not knowing how a search algorithm works makes it harder to understand what kinds of biases it contains. Clearing your browser history isn't a perfect fix but it may decrease the biasing information algorithms use.

In addition to algorithms, "bad actors" (people spreading disinformation on purpose) work to get false messages in front of users. They may pay money for advertising or hire people to troll the internet to spread disinformation. Messages often take advantage of the very biases you've learned about. Like distorting scientific findings and raising doubts about facts without providing evidence against it. Sometimes they just lie!

"Sticky" Messages

Misinformation and disinformation on the internet and social media can be extremely "sticky." That can make it difficult to correct. Think about what you've learned about false beliefs. Computers can supercharge all of them.

Fake experts	People pretending to have expertise
Anecdotes	One person's experience
Confirmation bias	Presenting information that fits what a person already believes
Automatic vigilance	Making people afraid or anxious
False consensus effect	The impression that the information is widely believed even if it isn't
Familiarity effect	The same message seen over and over again
Hidden motives	Anonymous sources may make money or get power from convincing others
A good story	Explanations based on disinformation or conspiracy theories

☀ CHECK OUT THE RESEARCH ☀

How can false ideas be corrected? You might have guessed by now that just providing facts is not enough to keep people from believing things that aren't true. Stephan Lewandowsky and others have looked at lots of research findings that found just that. These scientists used the phrase, "post-truth era" to describe our current time where misinformation and disinformation are so widespread that facts have lost some of their impact.

Real World Impact

Social media can be anonymous. Sometimes sources can be hard to determine. Things that are completely made up can sound true. When rumors or disinformation is about a group of people, it can spread hate and reinforce stereotypes. Angry messages can even encourage violent behavior.

Rapidly spreading misinformation and disinformation also make it harder for experts and governments to inform people. During the COVID-19 pandemic, false reports made some unwilling to wear masks and social distance. These false reports claimed the virus wasn't that bad. Other false reports said the government was trying to take away personal freedoms. Rumors about dangers from the vaccine discouraged some people from getting them. The result was unnecessary illness and death.

Now You Know

- The internet and social media allow for very rapid information sharing and contribute to false information going viral.

- The internet and social media have few controls over whether the information provided is true or false.

- Search engines use information about your prior searches online and contacts, and other online behavior to feed you information it predicts you'll like.

- How you search for information influences what you are likely to find.

CHAPTER 13

What Can You Do?

Magicians work hard to trick their audiences. But when you see a magician perform, you don't really think they pulled a coin from someone's ear or a rabbit from a hat. You knew before the show you'd be seeing things that looked real but weren't. If you read a fictional book or see a movie, you won't confuse it with the truth. It turns out knowing ahead of time that you'll see or hear something untrue protects you from being fooled! Just like with magic shows and fiction!

Loosening the Glue on "Sticky" Ideas

Changing ideas that people already believe is hard. But it's not impossible. Some things that most people believed in the past are no longer seen as true. As you learned in Chapter 11, most people (even doctors) once believed smoking cigarettes was healthy. The fact that few people see smoking as healthy nowadays demonstrates how beliefs can change. But how? Just providing facts isn't enough. But some of the same things that make false beliefs stick can be used to challenge them. If accurate information is repeated over and over, it can replace incorrect beliefs. Telling someone once that smoking causes cancer may not have worked. But running ads, putting warnings on cigarette packages, and having experts on TV repeat that message frequently for years helped convince people tobacco was dangerous.

Messages from trusted experts also help correct false ideas. Past ideas about the safety of smoking changed when people heard messages from scientists and their own doctors.

Try This

Think about the last movie you saw. What clues did you have that what you were seeing wasn't real? Consider the setting you were in. Think about comments of friends or others with you. What about the title of the movie or things you might have known about the actors? How about costumes, sets, technology in the film, special effects, or words presented at the beginning or end of the film?

Big changes in beliefs often start with very small steps. The idea of marriage equality used to be very unpopular. It was closely tied to untrue ideas about LGBTQ+ people. As people started to realize that gay people wanted the same things as they did, like being with a partner in a loving relationship, starting a family, and being part of the community, it was hard to deny anyone the right to marry whoever they wanted. People also began to realize they knew and cared about friends, co-workers, and even family members who are gay and loved people of their own gender. Knowing someone with similarities to yourself makes it harder to view others as outsiders. Once accurate understanding begins in small ways, it's easier to question related false ideas. So, small first steps can be crucial to moving closer to the truth.

Prebunking: warning in advance of false information to prevent misinformation or disinformation.

Another way to "unstick" incorrect information is to help someone see how they were misled in the first place. Telling people how and why they were given a false message makes them more open to hearing a different point of view. If they learn the initial story came from someone who had a reason to lie to them, they may think again about what they were told.

But one of the best ways to prevent people from accepting false information is to warn them it's coming! Just like magic tricks and fictional stories, knowing you're about to hear something false can keep you from believing it in the first place. Alerting people they are about to hear false information is called **prebunking**.

CHECK OUT THE RESEARCH

Psychologists Ullrich Ecker, Stephan Lewandowsky, and David Tang told people a story about a bus accident. One group was warned there would be some false details in the story. The other group didn't get that warning. Both groups heard that people on the bus were older adults. Later, everyone was told this was a mistake and the people were not older. Participants were also told it had been hard to get passengers out of the bus, even if they were uninjured.

The research participants were then asked why they thought people had trouble escaping the bus. People who had not gotten the prebunking warning said things like, "they were frail and weak." It didn't seem like they'd let go of the idea that the passengers were older adults (even though they had been told that wasn't true). The people who were warned about hearing some false facts gave reasons that didn't suggest the folks on the bus were older. Warning participants to be on the lookout for false information seemed to work!

Later in a follow-up study, these same researchers found another interesting detail about prebunking. If people were warned they would receive some false information and that it would later be corrected (like the bus was really carrying student athletes), the correction was even more effective.

So, when trying to correct misinformation and disinformation it's important that facts fit into a story that seems sensible. Giving people an explanation for why they got false information in the first place can help. Explaining why the original source was not trustworthy also helps.

Real World Impact

In 2021, Russia attacked Ukraine. The Russian government made fake videos to justify this invasion. They seemed to show Ukrainian soldiers had attacked Russians first. Fortunately, the United States learned about this plan. Before the Russian president could spread disinformation, the United States warned the world about these videos and how they had been made. This prebunking prevented Russia's president from convincing the world his attack on Ukraine had been justified.

Why Might Someone Hold Tight to a False Belief?

You've learned when someone hears something that contradicts what they believe they experience cognitive dissonance. They might think of reasons to reject the new message because of it. A corrective message can even backfire and make someone hold onto incorrect beliefs more tightly. So how do you help someone realize what they think is false? First, don't challenge their ideas. It is more effective to show them how the new information supports their values or goals.

EXPLORE FURTHER
Practice prebunking! Check out the online game at https://www.getbadnews.com/en and get some hands-on practice spotting misinformation and disinformation. The game was designed as a tool to show tricks used to spread falsehoods. Research shows it actually helps!

You are wrong!

Here are some facts that might help you get what you want.

CHECK OUT THE RESEARCH

You've learned about the false idea that measles vaccine caused autism. Zachary Horne and coworkers were interested in how to help parents understand this wasn't true. Their subjects were parents who were afraid to vaccinate their kids. The researchers knew that challenging false beliefs about the dangers of vaccines was ineffective or could even backfire. But they understood that fear of the vaccines came from parents' concern for their children's health. Instead of directly challenging the parents' false beliefs, the researchers wondered if helping them understand how vaccines could help their children would change their decisions.

They used three groups of adults. One group (the control group) got no information about vaccines. A second group was given information used by a government agency. The agency provided facts showing vaccines were safe and did not cause autism. The third group was given information about how many children had gotten sick or died from measles in the past. They also got information about how effective vaccines had been against this deadly disease. You may not be surprised to learn the last message given to group 3 was most effective in changing people's minds about vaccines.

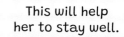

This will help her to stay well.

Guarding Against False Beliefs

You may be wondering how you can protect yourself from being convinced of things that aren't true. After all, it seems to happen a lot! Making mistakes about what is true and what is false happens to everyone. And it happens no matter how smart you are. But being aware of what might make you believe a falsehood makes you less likely to be fooled! Now that you know how misleading ideas are introduced and spread, it can help you question sources and accuracy of "facts" you come across. Knowing there are people who distort "facts" for their own purposes can help you recognize why someone might mislead you. Being aware of common techniques of disinformation can help you spot them. Recognizing logical fallacies can help you recognize twisted messages. Not falling for messages like everyone thinks a certain way, when it isn't true, or recognizing someone lying with statistics (such as percentages) can too.

Who says?

What did they say?

Why are they saying that?

Where's the proof?

Try This

Imagine you are running for president of your class. Your opponent says the school board is demanding all schools end spring and summer vacations. They also say they have a plan to stop them. But it's all a lie! How might you most effectively ensure students don't believe the lies? If they have already convinced people they can save vacations from the school board, how would you try to change this false belief?

Researchers Soroush Vosoughi, Deb Roy, and Sinan Aral found false information spread far more quickly on an online social media service called Twitter than the truth did. In fact, false stories were shared about 70% more than true ones. False news reached far more people than accurate news. Their study suggested this happened because the false stories were more surprising and more emotional.

Try This

A pencil and sharpener cost $1.10 together. If the pencil costs $1 more than the sharpener, what is the cost of the sharpener alone?

If you said the sharpener cost ten cents, you are a victim of fast thinking. No worries. You're not alone. Take a slower approach. Do you see where you went wrong? Still stumped? The answer is at the end of this chapter.

Slow Down and Think

Psychologist Daniel Kahneman suggests there are two ways of thinking: fast and slow. Fast thinking is automatic and happens in an instant. In fact, it usually happens without you realizing it. Fast thinking can lead to errors of perception, attention, memory, and bias, which you've read about earlier.

Slow thinking is more careful and rational. With a bit more time you can consider gaps or distortions that may exist in information. You can consider what might be affecting your first impressions. You can consider if the source of information is trustworthy. Slowing down is needed for **critical thinking**. It requires effort and awareness of how judgements can be wrong. You know, all the things you need to do to avoid believing things that aren't true!

Critical thinking: the process of analyzing evidence, arguments, and observations to form a judgement.

Thinking critically means questioning what you are being told. It means understanding where the information is coming from and thinking about what might be interfering with your ability to rationally process what you're hearing. It also means keeping in mind the kinds of things you've learned throughout this book.

Check it!

The source

Expert	VS	nonexpert, celebrity, or fake expert
Trusted	VS	motivated by money or power
Known	VS	unknown
Multiple trusted sources	VS	one person says so

The message

Evidence-based	VS	opinion, rumors, lies
Causation	VS	correlation only
Careful research	VS	anecdotes and testimonials
Logical	VS	not logical or twisted logic
Including lots of data	VS	cherry picking findings and incomplete graphs

Social pressures

Messages you feel free to decide about	VS	peer pressure
People really agree	VS	false consensus based on repetition

Your reaction to the message

Openness to new ideas	VS	cognitive dissonance
Calm emotions	VS	fear, anxiety, anger
Willingness to reconsider	VS	looking to confirm what you already think

You may be thinking, "WOW! That's too much to remember!" You're right! Learning to protect yourself from believing things that aren't true takes time. Think of it as building a new strength. As you practice questioning, it will become easier. Each time you take the small step of applying what you've learned, you'll take a giant leap toward becoming a...

CRITICAL THINKER!

Now You Know

- Knowing ahead of time that a message is false can prevent someone from believing it. This is why we don't believe fictional stories. This prebunking can also prevent people from being misled by disinformation.

- False beliefs can be very difficult, though not impossible, to change. Sometimes big changes in beliefs start with small steps.

- Addressing someone's values or goals can help reduce their cognitive dissonance.

- Thinking slowly and critically, and considering what you've learned throughout this book, can help protect you from misinformation and disinformation.

(BTW—that sharpener cost 5¢. The pencil cost $1.05.)

Glossary

A

Accuracy motivation: when a person searching for new information is working to understand what is true.

Adrenaline: a hormone that prepares your body for exertion by increasing breathing and blood flow.

Algorithm: a process or set of rules that a computer program follows to solve a problem.

Amygdala: a part of the brain involved with anger, fear, and memory.

Anecdote: a person's report about one experience.

Apophenia: perceiving patterns or meaning in meaningless data.

Artificial Intelligence (AI): human-like thinking processes done by computers.

Automatic vigilance: an unconscious fear response that leads people to look for danger. It can sometimes lead us to perceive threats that aren't real.

B

Base rates: how often something usually happens. This rate can be compared to the rate under experimental conditions.

Boomerang effect: the strengthening of old beliefs when challenged by new, more accurate information. This may cue the listener to think about arguments against the new data.

C

Causation: when one thing results in another thing happening.

Cherry picking: selecting data that seems to support one position and ignoring data that contradicts it.

Code switching: the name for changing your language, manner, or outward appearance depending on the social context and group you're in.

Cognitive consistency: when two ideas fit together.

Cognitive dissonance: when ideas don't fit together. Sometimes this causes us to be uncomfortable.

Confirmation bias: the tendency for people to seek out information that supports the views they already have.

Conformity: the tendency to change behavior and/or beliefs to fit in with a social group.

Conspiracy: a secret plot formed by two or more people.

Conspiracy theory: a theory suggesting a powerful group is keeping something hidden from the public or has caused an event to occur.

Continued-influence effect: a tendency for false information to continue to be believed even when it has been retracted (taken back) or corrected.

Control group: research participants who are similar to people in the experimental group, but do not get the experimental treatment.

Correlation: when two things tend to change together, although it's not clear if one causes the other or if they are both changed by something else.

Critical thinking: the process of analyzing evidence, arguments, and observations to form a judgement.

D

Directional motivation: when a person seeking new information is only interested in what fits what they already believe.

Disinformation: purposeful misinformation. Falsehoods are deliberately spread to deceive others. Often people spreading disinformation can profit financially, professionally, or politically.

Dunning-Kruger effect: when people with limited knowledge or skills in an area tend to overestimate their knowledge and underestimate what they don't know.

E

Emotion: the sense people make of, and the labels they use, to understand bodily sensations in a given situation.

Evidence-based: conclusions based on systematic methods of data collection. Often, this is through a collection of scientific studies.

Experiment: a scientific test of a hypothesis.

Experimental group: research participants who are subjected to an experimental procedure to test a hypothesis.

F

Fact: a conclusion based on evidence.

Failure to replicate: when a research study is repeated by others but fails to find the original results.

Fake experts: unqualified sources of information.

False consensus effect: the tendency to overestimate how many other people share our beliefs.

Familiarity bias: when we accept familiar ideas without careful thought about their accuracy.

Functional magnetic resonance imagery (fMRI): brain imagery that uses magnetic technology to map brain activity.

G

Gatekeeping: the process of selecting and filtering information before it is presented to the public.

Generalization: a conclusion that something is true in most cases. It's not wise to make generalizations based on evidence from one or a few specific cases.

Gestalt principles: laws that describe how humans recognize patterns, simplify images, and group information to aid in perception of objects. Like the **law of continuity** that says we tend to see broken lines as unbroken, or the **closure principle** that says we fill in a set of curved, but unattached, lines to form a circle.

H

Hypothalamus: a part of your brain that regulates many bodily functions.

Hypothesis: an idea or possible explanation for something that has been observed and is tested through experimentation.

I

Identity: how a person sees themself, including where they fit in with others, their social roles, and their relationships.

Implicit bias: an unconscious negative reaction to (or preference for) a person or a group.

Inattentional blindness: the failure to see something that is clearly visible because attention is focused on another activity or object.

IQ: standing for "Intelligence Quotient," this measurement is based on a set of tests designed to measure how well someone can think and learn.

L

Leveling: the process of simplifying details of a story to make it easier to remember.

Lie: an untrue statement designed to mislead someone.

Logical fallacy: an argument drawing on incomplete evidence to reach a conclusion that sounds sensible but isn't logical.

M

Misinformation: incorrect or misleading information that can result in others being misinformed. Misinformation may be spread without the intention to mislead other people.

Misperception: a mistaken or untrue impression about something.

Myth: an idea, often in the form of a story, that is widely believed but untrue. Myths are sometimes repeated through generations.

O

Opinion: a thought or judgement that isn't based on evidence.

P

Pareidolia: the tendency to see recognizable objects or patterns in random visual displays.

Peer review: when research is evaluated by other professionals with expertise in a given field. For scientific research, this includes deciding if proper research methods were used and if conclusions are consistent with reported data.

Perception: the recognition and interpretation of sensory information.

Population: in a research study, the larger community group the researcher is trying to learn about.

Positive feedback: information indicating a behavior is working, making it more likely someone will do it again.

Prebunking: warning in advance of false information to prevent misinformation or disinformation.

R

Reliable: a person or information that is trustworthy.

Replication: repeating a research study another scientist did to see if the same results happen.

Representative sample: a sample from a larger group that accurately mirrors the larger population of interest.

Rumor: a story or statement passed from person to person without evidence about whether it is true or invented.

S

Sample: the group of people who participate in a survey or research experiment.

Sampling bias: the result of choosing research participants who do not represent a wide variety of people.

Scientific method: using systematic observation, measurement, and experimentation to form and test hypotheses.

Secondhand information: information that is learned from someone else.

Self-fulfilling prophecy: when you believe others' false ideas about you or your skills and change your behavior to fit their expectations.

Senses/Sensory organs: our five senses are sight, hearing, touch, taste, and smell. Information is collected through sensory organs (eyes, ears, skin and pressure sensors, taste buds, and nose) and sent to the brain for interpretation.

Sharpening: the process of focusing on the most interesting parts of a story and leaving out details.

Social norms: the informal rules of accepted behavior, attitudes, and beliefs of a culture or social group.

Source: where something comes from. This can include a person, news article, book, or video that provides information.

Statistical significance: a measure (using math) that makes it seem sensible to accept results of an experiment as being more than just chance.

Stereotypes: preconceived ideas about the typical preferences, beliefs, and behaviors of a group of people, and individuals within that group.

Survey: a list of questions aimed at gaining information about a particular topic.

T

Testimonial: a person's report about the value or usefulness of something.

Theory: a carefully considered explanation for something, based on observation and prior knowledge.

U

Urban myth: a strange or shocking falsehood that isn't true but is widely known and shared.

Bibliography

BOOKS

Chabris, C. & Simons, D. (2009). *The invisible gorilla: How our intuitions deceive us*. Crown Publishing Group.

Festinger, L., Riecken, H. W., & Schacter, S. (2009). *When prophecy fails: A social and psychological study of a modern group that predicted the destruction of the world*. Mansfield Center.

Gilovich, T. (1991). *How we know what isn't so: The fallibility of human reason in everyday life.* The Free Press.

Gilovich, T., & Ross, L. (2015). *The wisest one in the room: How you can benefit from social psychology's most powerful insights.* The Free Press.

Kahneman, D. (2011). *Thinking, fast and slow (1st ed.).* Straus and Giroux.

Sharot, T. (2017). *The influential mind: What the brain reveals about our power to change others*. Henry Holt and Co.

Sinatra, G. M., & Hofer, B. K. (2021). *Science denial: Why it happens and what to do about it.* Oxford University Press.

Vyse, S. (2014). *Believing in magic: The psychology of superstition.* Oxford University Press.

OTHER REFERENCES
INTRO

American Family Care. (n.d.). *Cold and flu myth busters.* https://www.afcurgentcare.com/blog/cold-and-flu-myth-busters/

Blakemore, E. (2023, August 10). *Christopher Columbus never set out to prove the Earth was round.* History. https://www.history.com/news/christopher-columbus-never-set-out-to-prove-the-earth-was-round

Borel, B. (2012, February 6). *Why do bulls charge when they see red?* LiveScience. https://www.livescience.com/33700-bulls-charge-red.html

Chew, S. L., (2018, August 29). *Myth: We only use 10% of our brains.* Association for Psychological Science. https://www.psychologicalscience.org/uncategorized/myth-we-only-use-10-of-our-brains.html

Duke Health (2013, August 26). *Myth or fact: Should you wait to swim after eating?* https://www.dukehealth.org/blog/myth-or-fact-should-you-wait-swim-after-eating#:~:text=The%20common%20belief%20that%20the,According%20to%20Dr.

Gibbens, S. (2019, January 23). *Why cold weather doesn't mean climate change is fake.* National Geographic. https://www.nationalgeographic.com/environment/article/climate-change-colder-winters-global-warming-polar-vortex

Hammond, C. (2012, October 1). *Is reading in the dark bad for your eyesight?* BBC. https://www.bbc.com/future/article/20121001-should-you-read-in-the-dark

Hodgeback, J. (n.d.). *Are bats really blind?* Britannica. https://www.britannica.com/story/are-bats-really-blind

Lieber, A. (2015, August 8). *How do dogs sweat?* PetPlace. https://www.petplace.com/article/dogs/pet-behavior-training/how-do-dogs-sweat/

Moncel, B. (2019, October 2). T*he twinkie myth.* The Spruce Eats. https://www.thespruceeats.com/the-twinkie-myth-1328772

NOAA. (2020, August 19). *5 striking facts versus myths about lightning you should know.* https://www.noaa.gov/stories/5-striking-facts-versus-myths-about-lightning-you-should-know

Smith, K.A., (2013, June 18). *Why the tomato was feared in Europe for more than 200 years.* Smithsonian. https://www.smithsonianmag.com/arts-culture/why-the-tomato-was-feared-in-europe-for-more-than-200-years-863735/

CHAPTER ONE

Brewer, W. F., & Treyens, J. C. (1981). Role of schemata in memory for places. *Cognitive Psychology*, *13*(2), 207–230. https://doi.org/10.1016/0010-0285(81)90008-6

Elbein, A. (2021, March 10). Tasmanian tigers are extinct. Why do people keep seeing them? *The New York Times*. https://www.nytimes.com/2021/03/10/science/thylacines-tasmanian-tigers-sightings.html

Garry, M., French, L., Kinzett, T., & Mori, K. (2007, August 9). Eyewitness memory following discussion: using the MORI technique with a Western sample. *Applied Cognitive Psychology*, *22*(4), 431–439.

Kashino, M. (2006, November). Phonemic restoration: The brain creates missing speech sounds. *Acoustical Science and Technology*, *27*(6), 318-321. https://doi.org/10.1250/ast.27.318

Simons, D.J., & Chabris, C.F. (1999). Gorillas in our midst: Sustained inattentional blindness for dynamic events. *Perception*, *28*(9), 1059–1074.

CHAPTER TWO

Arnocky, S., Bozek, E., Dufort, C., Rybka, S., & Hebert, R. (2018). Celebrity opinion influences public acceptance of human evolution. *Evolutionary Psychology*, *16*(3). https://doi.org/10.1177/1474704918800656

Meshi, D., Biele, G., Korn, C. W., & Heekeren, H. R. (2012). How expert advice influences decision making. *PLoS One*, *7*(11): e49748. https://doi.org/10.1371/journal.pone.0049748

Wade, K. A., Garry, M., Don Read, J. D., et al. (2002). A picture is worth a thousand lies: Using false photographs to create false childhood memories. *Psychonomic Bulletin & Review*, 9, 597–603. https://doi.org/10.3758/BF03196318

CHAPTER THREE

Crair, B. (2018, September). Why do so many people still want to believe in Bigfoot? *Smithsonian Magazine*. https://www.smithsonianmag.com/history/why-so-many-people-still-believe-in-bigfoot-180970045/

Gilbert, D. T., Krull, D. S., & Malone, P. S. (1990). Unbelieving the unbelievable: Some problems in the rejection of false information. *American Psychological Association*, *59*(4), 601–613.

Gilovich, T. (1987, January). Secondhand information and social judgement. *Journal of Experimental Social Psychology*, *23*(1), 59–74.

Hasson, U. (2016, June 3). *This is your brain on communication* [Video]. TED Conferences. https://www.youtube.com/watch?v=FDhlOovaGrl

Hasson, U. (2019, October). *Storytelling and memories: How the act of storytelling shapes our minds.* iBiology. https://www.ibiology.org/neuroscience/storytelling-and-memories/#part-2

Mangan, D. (2019, June 5). *He got the FBI to test 'Bigfoot' hair in the 1970s and this 93-year-old man is still searching for Sasquatch.* CNBC. https://www.cnbc.com/2019/06/05/fbi-tested-bigfoot-hair-in-1970s-government-documents-show.html

National Geographic Kids (n.d.) *Ancient 'unicorns' may have roamed Earth with humans!* https://www.natgeokids.com/uk/discover/animals/prehistoric-animals/siberian-unicorn-fossil-discovery-humans/#:~:text=A%20ground%2Dbreaking%20fossil%20discovery,skull%20was%20found%20in%20Kazakhstan

Renken, E. (2020, April 11). *How stories connect and persuade us: Unleashing the brain power of narrative.* NPR. https://www.npr.org/sections/health-shots/2020/ 04/11/815573198/how-stories-connect-and-persuade-us-unleashing-the-brain-power-of-narrative

CHAPTER FOUR

Armellino, D., Hussain, E., Schilling, M. E., Senicola, W., Eichorn, A., Dlugacz, Y., & Farber, B. F. (2011). Using high-technology to enforce low-technology safety measures: The use of third-party remote video auditing and real-time feedback in healthcare. *Clinical Infectious Diseases*, *54*(1), 1–7.

Cacioppo, J. T., Priester, J. R., & Berntson, G. G. (1993). Rudimentary determinants of attitudes: II. Arm flexion and extension have differential effects on attitudes. *Journal of Personality and Social Psychology*, *65*(1), 5–17. https://doi.org/10.1037/0022-3514.65.1.5

EPA (2023, February 2). *Brown marmorated stink bug.* https://www.epa.gov/safepestcontrol/brown-marmorated-stink-bug#:~:text=The%20brown%20marmorated%20stink%20bug,away%20in%20a%20shipping%20container

Garrett N., González-Garzón A. M., Foulkes L., Levita L., Sharot T. (2018). *Updating beliefs under perceived threat.* J*ournal of Neuroscience*, *38*(36):7901–7911. https://doi:10.1523/JNEUROSCI.0716-18.2018. Epub 2018 Aug 6. PMID: 30082420; PMCID: PMC6125815

Hermans, D., De Houwer, J., & Eelen, P. (2001). A time course analysis of the affective priming effect. *Cognition and Emotion*, *15*(2), 143–165. https://doi.org/10.1080/0269993004200033

Kahneman, D., Tversky, A. (1979). Prospect theory: An analysis of decision under risk. *Econometrica*, *47*(2), 263–291.

Larsen, R. J. (2004, November 1). *Emotion and cognition: The case of automatic vigilance*. Psychological Science Agenda. https://www.apa.org/science/about/psa/2004/11/larsen

Payne, B. K. (2001). Prejudice and perception: The role of automatic and controlled processes in misperceiving a weapon. *Journal of Personality and Social Psychology, 81*(2), 181–192. https://doi.org/10.1037/0022-3514.81.2.181

Risen, J. L., & Critcher, C. R. (2011). Visceral fit: While in a visceral state, associated states of the world seem more likely. *Journal of Personality and Social Psychology, 100*(5), 777–793. https://doi.org/10.1037/a0022460

Schwartz, A. B. (2015, May 6). The infamous "War of the Worlds" radio broadcast was a magnificent fluke. *Smithsonian Magazine*. https://www.smithsonianmag.com/history/infamous-war-worlds-radio-broadcast-was-magnificent-fluke-180955180/

Suttie, J. (2020, September 3). Eight ways your perception of reality is skewed. *Greater Good Magazine*. https://greatergood.berkeley.edu/article/item/eight_reasons_to_distrust_your_own_perceptions

Vedantam, S. (Host). (2017, March 13*). Hidden brain: When it comes to politics and 'fake news,' facts aren't enough.* [Audio podcast]. https://www.npr.org/2017/03/13/519661419/when-it-comes-to-politics-and-fake-news-facts-arent-enough

Weihenmayer, Erik. (2023). *No barriers climb program*. https://erikweihenmayer.com/no-barriers-climb-program/

Wells, G. L., & Petty, R. E. (1980). The effects of over head movements on persuasion: Compatibility and incompatibility of responses. *Basic and Applied Social Psychology, 1*(3), 219–230. https://doi.org/10.1207/s15324834basp0103_2

CHAPTER FIVE

Festinger, L., & Carlsmith, J. M. (1959). Cognitive consequences of forced compliance. *Journal of Abnormal and Social Psychology, 58*(2), 203–210. https://doi.org/10.1037/h0041593

Festinger, L., Riecken, H. W., & Schachter, S. (1956). *When prophecy fails.* University of Minnesota Press.

Harmon-Jones, E., & Mills, J. (2019). An introduction to cognitive dissonance theory and an overview of current perspectives on the theory. In E. Harmon-Jones (Ed.), *Cognitive dissonance: Reexamining a pivotal theory in psychology* (pp. 3–24). American Psychological Association. https://doi.org/10.1037/0000135-001

Kahneman, D. (2011). *Thinking, fast and slow* (1st ed.). Straus and Giroux.

Lepper, M. R., Greene, D., & Nisbett, R. E. (1973). Undermining children's intrinsic interest with extrinsic reward: A test of the overjustification hypothesis. *Journal of Personality and Social Psychology, 28*(1), 129–37.

Rice, J. (2021, August 21). *16 weirdest foods of the world.* Rough Guides. https://www.roughguides.com/gallery/weird-food/

Ruhl, C. (2020, December 1). *The Stroop effect.* Simply Psychology. https://www.simplypsychology.org/stroop-effect.html

Shaw, D. (n.d.). *17 surprising facts about snow.* BBC Earth. https://www.bbcearth.com/news/17-surprising-facts-about-snow

Sunstein, C., Lazzaro, S., & Sharot, T. (2016). How people update beliefs about climate change: Good news and bad news. *SSRN Electronic Journal*, *102*(6). https://www.researchgate.net/publication/315487933_How_People_Update_Beliefs_about_Climate_Change_Good_News_and_Bad_News

Travel Food Atlas (2018, November 18). *45 weirdest foods around the world.* https://travelfoodatlas.com/weirdest-foods-eaten-around-world

Zajonc, R. B. & Rajecki, D. W. (1969). Exposure and affect: A field experiment. *Psychonomic Science*, *17*(4), 216–217. https://doi.org/10.3758/BF03329178

CHAPTER SIX

Crocker, J. (1982). Biased questions in judgment of covariation studies. *Personality and Social Psychology Bulletin*, *8*(2), 214–220. https://journals.sagepub.com/doi/10.1177/0146167282082005

Festinger, L., Riecken, H. W., & Schachter, S. (1956). *When prophecy fails.* University of Minnesota Press.

Martinez, A., & Christnacht, C. (2021, January 26). *Women are nearly half of U.S. workforce but only 27% of STEM workers.* United States Census Bureau. https://www.census.gov/library/stories/2021/01/women-making-gains-in-stem-occupations- but-still-underrepresented.html

Rosenthal, R., & Jacobson, L. (1968). *Pygmalion in the classroon: Teacher expectation and pupils' intellectual development.* Holt, Rinehart & Winston.

Wason, P. C. (1960). On the failure to eliminate hypotheses in a conceptual task. *QuarterlyJournal of Experimental Psychology*, *12*(3), 129–140. https://doi.org/10.1080/17470216008416717

CHAPTER SEVEN

Asch, S. E. (1951). Effects of group pressure upon the modification and distortion of judgments. In H. Guetzkow (Ed.), *Groups, leadership and men; research in human relations*, 177–190. Carnegie Press.

Bateson, M., Nettle, D., & Roberts, G. (2006). Cues of being watched enhance cooperation in a real-world setting. *Biol Lett*, *2*(3), 412–414. DOI: 10.1098/rsbl.2006.0509

Baumeister, R. F., & Leary, M. R. (1995). The need to belong: Desire for interpersonal attachments as a fundamental human motivation. *Psychology Bulletin*, *117*(3), 497–529. https://doi.org/10.1037/0033-2909.117.3.497

Busting the sugar-hyperactivity myth. (1999). *Grow by WebMD.* https://www.webmd.com/parenting/features/busting-sugar-hyperactivity-myth#1

Charpentier, C. J., Moutsiana, C., Garrett, N., & Sharot, T. (2014, April 23). The brain's temporal dynamics from a collective decision to individual action. *Journal of Neuroscience*, *34*(17), 5816–5823. DOI: https://doi.org/10.1523/JNEUROSCI.4107-13.2014

Dr. Seuss, (1961). *Sneetches and other stories.* Random House.

Jenness, A. (1932). The role of discussion in changing opinion regarding a matter of fact. *The Journal of Abnormal and Social Psychology*, *27*(3), 279–296. https://doi.org/10.1037/h0074620

Lewandowsky, S., Ecker, U., & Cook, J. (2017). Beyond misinformation: Understanding and coping with the "post-truth" era. *Journal of Applied Research in Memory and Cognition*, *6*(4), 353–369. DOI:10.1016/j.jarmac.2017.07.008

Livingston, A., & Zou, I. (2021, July 2). State museum canceled book event examining slavery's role in Battle of the Alamo after Texas GOP leaders complained, authors say. *Texas Tribune*. https://www.texastribune.org/2021/07/01/texas-forget-the-alamo-book-event-canceled/

McCluney, C., Robotham, K., Lee, S., Smith, R., & Durkee, M. (2019, November 15). *The costs of code-switching*. Harvard Business Review. https://hbr.org/2019/11/the-costs-of-codeswitching

Otteson, K.K. (2021, December 27).Greta Thunberg on the state of the climate movement. *The Washington Post Magazine*. https://www.washingtonpost.com/magazine/2021/12/27greta-thunberg-state-climate-movement-roots-her-power-an-activist/

Sundie, J. M., Cialdini, R. B., Griskevicius, V., & Kendrick, D. T. (2012). The world's (truly) oldest profession: Social influence in evolutionary perspective. *Social Influence*, *7*(3), 134–153. DOI: 10.1080/15534510.2011.649890

Thompson, M. (2013, April 13). *Five reasons why people code-switch*. NPR. https://www.npr.org/sections/codeswitch/2013/04/13/177126294/five-reasons-why-people-code-switch

Wolraich, M. L., Wilson, D., & White, J. W. (1995). The effect of sugar on behavior or cognition in children: A meta-analysis. *JAMA*, *274*(20), 1617–1621. doi:10:1001/jama.1995.03530200053037

CHAPTER EIGHT

Barkman, R. C. (2018, January 18). *See the world through patterns: When you see them, they can be life-changing.* Psychology Today. https://www.psychologytoday.com/us/blog/singular-perspective/201801/see-the-world-throughpatterns#:~:text=Pattern%20recognition%20according%20to%20IQ,factor%20(Kurzweil%2C%202012

Earth Sky Voices. (2022, November 25). *Seeing things that aren't there? It's called pareidolia.* Earth Sky. https://earthsky.org/human-world/seeing-things-that-arent-there/

Husted, K. (2011). *Can Frequent Family Dinners Help Teens Resist Drugs?* NPR. https://www.npr.org/sections/health-shots/2011/09/22/140705512/can-frequent-family-dinners-help-teens-resist-drugs

Jones, E. (2015, September 16). The Fun Theory. *SiOWfa15: Science in Our World: Certainty and Controversy.* https://sites.psu.edu/siowfa15/2015/09/16/the-fun-theory/

Master Class. (2021, June 7). *Apophenia explained: How to avoid apophenia bias.* https://www.masterclass.com/articles/how-to-avoid-apophenia-bias#4-types-of -apophenia

Morse, M. S. (1997, October). Facing a bumpy history. *Smithsonian Magazine.* https://www.smithsonianmag.com/history/facing-a-bumpy-history-144497373/

Zach. (2021, August 18). *Correlation does not imply caustion: 5 real-world examples.* Statology. https://www.statology.org/correlation-does-not-imply-causation-examples/

CHAPTER NINE

Asch, S. E. (1946). Forming impressions of personality. *The Journal of Abnormal and Social Psychology, 41*(3), 258–290. https://doi.org/10.1037/h0055756

Chabris, C., & Simons, D. (2009). *The invisible gorilla: How our intuitions deceive us.* Crown Publishing Group.

Howard-Jones, P. (2014, October). *Neuroscience and education: Myths and messages.* Nature Reviews Neuroscience, 15. https://www.researchgate.net/publication/266945518_Neuroscience_and_education_Myths_and_messages

Johnson, H. M., & Seifert, C. M. (1994). Sources of the continued influence effect: When misinformation in memory affects later inferences. *Journal of Experimental Psychology: Learning, Memory, and Cognition, 20*(6), 1420–1436. https://doi.org/10.1037/0278 -7393.20.6.1420

Lamanna, M. (n.d.). *The two-headed dinosaur.* Carnegie Museum of Natural History. https://carnegiemnh.org/the-two-headed-dinosaur/

Lemonick, M. D. (2014, September 26). The people have voted: Pluto is a planet! *Time Magazine.* https://time.com/3429938/pluto-planet-vote/

Parsons, K. M. (n.d.). *The wrongheaded dinosaur.* Carnegie Museum of Natural History. https://carnegiemuseums.org/magazine-archive/1997/novdec/feat5.htm

Rao, T. S., & Adrade, C. (2011). The MMR vaccine and autism: Sensation, refutation, retraction, and fraud. *Indian Journal of Psychiatry, 53*(2), 95–96. https://doi.org/10.4103/0019-5545.82529

Stern, V. (2015, September 1). *A short history of the rise, fall and rise of subliminal messaging.* Scientific American. https://www.scientificamerican.com/article/a-short-history-of-the-rise-fall-and-rise-of-subliminal-messaging/

CHAPTER TEN

Bago, R., Rand, D. G., & Pennycook, G. (2020). Fake news, fast and slow: Deliberation reduces belief in false (but not true) news headlines. *Journal of Experimental Psychology: General, 149*(8), 1608–1613. http://dx.doi.org/10.1037/xge0000729

Berger, J. (2011, April 18). Arousal increases social transmission of information. *Psychological Science, 22*(7), 891–893. https://jonahberger.com/wpcontent/uploads/2013/02/Arousal2.pdf

Cherry, K. (2022, November 8). *What is the Dunning-Kruger effect?* Verywell mind. https://www.verywellmind.com/an-overview-of-the-dunning-kruger-effect-4160740

Curtin, C. (2007, January 4). *Fact or fiction?: Urinating on a jellyfish sting is an effective treatment.* Scientific American. https://www.scientificamerican.com/article/fact-or-fiction-urinating/

Douglas, K., Sutton, R. M., & Cichocka, A. (2017). *The psychology of conspiracy theories. Current Directions in Psychological Science, 26*(6), 538–542. https://journals.sagepub.com/doi/pdf/10.1177/0963721417718261

Dunning, D. (2011). The Dunning-Kruger effect: On being ignorant of one's own ignorance. *Advances in Experimental Psychology, 44*, 247–296. Academic Press. https://doi.org/10.1016/B978-0-12-385522-0.00005-6

Eveleth, R. (2011, Dec 6). *Do birds really abandon their chicks if humans touch them?* LiveScience. https://www.livescience.com/33620-baby-bird-touch-mother-abandon.html

Hall, M. P., & Raimi, K. T. (2018, May). Is belief superiority justified by superior knowledge? *Journal of Experimental Social Psychology, 76*, 290–306. https://doi.org/10.1016/j.jesp.2018.03.001

Jennings, K. (2013, August). *The Debunker. Do bananas grow on trees?* Woot! https://www.woot.com/blog/post/the-debunker-do-bananas-grow-on-trees

Lorenz, T. (2021, December 9). Birds aren't real, or are they? Inside a Gen Z conspiracy theory. *The New York Times.* https://www.nytimes.com/2021/12/09/technology/birds-arent-real-gen-z-misinformation.html

Meyers, H. (2021, December 7). *Can dogs see color?* American Kennel Club. https://www.akc.org/expert-advice/health/can-dogs-see-color/

NASA (2005, May 9). *China's wall less great in view from space.* https://www.nasa.gov/vision/space/workinginspace/great_wall.html

Pappas, S., & Radford, B. (2022, November 2). *16 of the best conspiracy theories.* LiveScience. https://www.livescience.com/11375-top-ten-conspiracy-theories.html

Thompson, D. (2021, January 29). *Anti-vaxxers wage campaigns against COVID-19 shots.* WebMD. https://www.webmd.com/vaccines/covid-19-vaccine/news/20210129/anti-vaxxers-mounting-internet-campaigns-against-covid-19-shots

Weill, K. (2022, February 27). *When your friends fall off the edge of the Earth.* The Atlantic. https://www.theatlantic.com/family/archive/2022/02/flat-earther-social-isolation/622908/

CHAPTER 11

AVMA (n.d.). *Why breed-specific legislation is not the answer.* https://www.avma.org/resources/pet-owners/why-breed-specific-legislation-not-answer

Bergstrom, C. T., & West, J. D. (2020). *Calling bullshit: The art of skepticism in a data-driven world.* Random House.

Cook, J. (2020, March 24). *A history of FLICC: The 5 techniques of science denial.* Cranky Uncle. https://crankyuncle.com/a-history-of-flicc-the-5-techniques-of-science-denial/

Domonoske, C. (2016, November 23). *Students have 'dismaying' inability to tell fake news from real, study finds.* NPR. https://www.npr.org/sections/the-two-way/2016/11/23/503129818/study-finds-students-have-dismaying-inability-to-tell-fake-news-from-real

Fein, S., McCloskey, A. L., & Tomlinson, T. M. (1997). Can the jury disregard that information? The use of suspicion to reduce the prejudicial effects of pretrial publicity and inadmissible testimony. *Personality and Social Psychology Bulletin, 23*(11), 1215–1226. https://doi.org/10.1177/01461672972311008

Gardner, M. N., & Brandt, A. M. (2006). "The doctors' choice is America's choice": The physician in US cigarette advertisements, 1930–1953. *American Journal of Public Health, 96*(2), 222–232. https://doi.org/10.2105/AJPH.2005.066654

Harper, N. (2020, December 17). *No, you're not 'just asking questions.' You're spreading disinformation*. Minnesota Reformer. https://minnesotareformer.com/2020/12/17/no-youre-not-just-asking-questions-youre-spreading-disinformation/

Hill, K., & White, J. (2020, November 21). Designed to deceive: Do these people look real to you? *The New York Times*. https://www.nytimes.com/interactive/2020/11/21/science/artificial-intelligence-fake-people-faces.html

LaCapria, K. (2017, February 2). *Did police raid and burn a Standing Rock protest camp?* Snopes. https://www.snopes.com/fact-check/police-burn-standing-rock-camp/

Lewandowsky, S., Ecker, U. K. H., Seifert, C. M., Schwarz, N., & Cook, J. (2012). Misinformation and its correction: Continued influence and successful debiasing. *Psychological Science in the Public Interest, 13*(3), 106–131. https://doi.org/10.1177/1529100612451018

Phillips, A. (2016, September 15). That time Congress railed against Dr. Oz for his 'miracle' diet pills. *The Washington Post*. https://www.washingtonpost.com/news/the-fix/wp/2016/09/15/that-time-congress-railed-on-dr-oz-for-his-miracle-diet-pills/

Readfearn, G. (2011, January 6). *A sunrise climate cock-up and reading cat's paws*. Graham Readfearn. https://www.readfearn.com/2011/01/a-sunrise-climate-cock-up-and-reading-cats-paws/

Tilbert, J. C., Allyse, M., & Hafferty, F. W. (2017, February). The case of Dr. Oz: Ethics, evidence, and does professional self-regulation work? *AMA Journal of Ethics, 19*(2), 199–206. https://journalofethics.ama-assn.org/article/case-dr-oz-ethics-evidence-and-does-professional-self-regulation-work/2017-02

CHAPTER TWELVE

Druckman, J., & McGrath, M. (2019, February). *The evidence for motivated reasoning in climate change preference formation*. Nature Climate Change, 9, 111–119.

Frenkel, S. (2021, July 24). The most influential spreader of coronavirus misinformation online. *The New York Times*. https://www.nytimes.com/2021/07/24/technology/joseph-mercola-coronavirus-misinformation-online.html

Jolley, D., & Douglas, K. M. (2014, February). The social consequences of conspiracism: Exposure to conspiracy theories decreases intentions to engage in politics and to reduce one's carbon footprint. *British Journal of Psychology, 105*(1), 35–56. https://doi.org/10.1111/bjop.12018

Kahan, D., Peters, E., Cantrell Dawson, E., & Slovic, P. (2017). Motivated numeracy and enlightened self-government. *Behavioural Public Policy, 1*(1), 54–86. doi:10.1017/bpp.2016.2

Lewandowsky, S., Ecker, U., & Cook, J. (2017, December). Beyond misinformation: Understanding and coping with the "post-truth" era. *Journal of Applied Research in Memory and Cognition, 6*(4), 353–369. DOI:10.1016/j.jarmac.2017.07.008

Rasmussen, C. (2021, November 9). *Emissions reductions from pandemic had unexpected effects on atmosphere.* NASA Jet Propulsion Laboratory. https://www.jpl.nasa.gov/news/emission-reductions-from-pandemic-had-unexpected-effects-on-atmosphere

Robb, A. (2017, November 16). *Anatomy of a fake news scandal.* Rolling Stone. https://www.rollingstone.com/feature/anatomy-of-a-fake-news-scandal-125877/

Samuelson, K. (2016, December 5). *What to know about Pizzagate, the fake news story with real consequences.* Time. https://time.com/4590255/pizzagate-fake-news-what-to-know/

CHAPTER THIRTEEN

Barnes, J. E. (2022, February 3). U.S. exposes what it says is Russian effort to fabricate pretext for invasion. *The New York Times.* https://www.nytimes.com/2022/02/03/us/politics/russia-ukraine-invasion-pretext.html

Ecker, U. K., Lewandowsky, S., & Tang, D. T. (2010). Explicit warnings reduce but do not eliminate the continued influence of misinformation. *Memory & Cognition, 38*(8), 1087–1100. https://doi.org/10.3758/MC.38.8.1087

Horne, Z., Powell, D., Hummel, J.E., & Holyoak, K. J. (2015, August 18). Countering antivaccination attitudes. *PNAS Proceedings of the National Academy of Sciences of the United States of America, 112*(33), 10321–10324. https://doi.org/10.1073/pnas.1504019112

Nolan, S. A., & Kimball, M. (2021, August 27). *What is prebunking?* Psychology Today. https://www.psychologytoday.com/us/blog/misinformation-desk/202108/what-is-prebunking

Vosoughi, S., Roy, D., & Aral, S. (2018, March 9). The spread of true and false news online. *Science, 359*(6380), 1146–1151. https://www.science.org/doi/10.1126/science.aap9559

Index

Acknowledgments

I have been so fortunate to have an editor who shares my passion for science and respect for bright and curious young readers. Thank you, Kristine Enderle. I am also grateful to the rest of the staff at Magination Press. Thanks for all you do, even the things I don't know about! Kaitlin Raimi, PhD and Brian Weeks, PhD at the University of Michigan offered suggestions and direction in my early research efforts. Thanks to both of you. My son-in-law, Matt Barrett, provided quick help with all computer glitches. Ever thankful and…you're not off the hook! Special thanks to my husband, Eric. Ever supportive, his companionship and lunch breaks made writing during pandemic isolation productive.

About the Author

Jacqueline B. Toner, PhD is a retired clinical psychologist with over 30 years in private practice working with children and parents. She earned her PhD from University of Virginia and served as Chief Facilitator for a medical resources project with Johns Hopkins School of Public Health and Carnegie Mellon University. Dr. Toner has co-authored several books with Claire A. B. Freeland, PhD, including three books in the What-To-Do Guides for Kids series as well as *Psychology For Kids: The Science of the Mind and Behavior*, *Depression: A Teen's Guide to Survive and Thrive* and *Yes I Can: A Girl and Her Wheelchair*. She lives in Baltimore, Maryland.

Visit www.jacquelinetoner.net